LIFE WITHOUT ME

Anna Legat

Published by Accent Press Ltd 2015

ISBN 9781783759521

Copyright © **Anna Legat** 2015

THE SUMMONS ...

I didn't see it coming. Had I done so, the shock alone would have killed me.

I didn't know what hit me, but it hit me hard.

I heard my skull crack as it slammed against the pavement. I had heard something similar once before, when my tooth broke on the shell of a small but nasty pistachio. It was one of those tough nuts, the last one in the bag, the one you're best advised to leave alone. It had a narrow hairline crack hinting at an opening, so I bit into it and that was when my canine split open and an electric current of pain travelled to my brain.

This time it wasn't my tooth, it was my skull. And this was far worse. My skull felt as if somebody else's teeth had crushed it to splinters. It felt as if its contents had poured out of my nose. Something certainly did. It could have been blood. It was warm.

I should have passed out, but I hung on to consciousness, wondering who would take care of all my unfinished business while doctors were trying to glue my brains together in the hospital. Who would take care of Mother? Emma? Mark? And who on earth would take care of Rob – because it certainly wouldn't be Rob.

My head had rolled awkwardly to face the house so I could see him pounce to the window. His mouth rounded in a scream which I couldn't hear, but I knew he definitely wouldn't hear me when I said, 'Don't just stand there! Call an ambulance!'

Though I couldn't hear myself say it either, so maybe I only thought it.

He ran out of the house with a kettle in his hand. I had always believed that people dropped things when in shock. Traditionally, the thing to drop would be a cup of tea; it would tumble slow-motion to the floor and smash into a thousand ceramic shards. A dramatic ping and the shocked person's face, frozen in horror, would complete the picture. Rob, however, had a different take on the matter. He was running towards me, clutching the bloody kettle with the cord dragging behind it on the ground. I heard the clanking of it. I heard Rob yell, 'Georgie!'

I gave up. I can't remember closing my eyes, but I stopped seeing. My hearing was gone too. I could hear and see nothing. Absolutely nothing! Not even a dark tunnel with a shimmer of light at the end of it.

I thought I was dead, but I wasn't. Not quite. At least not until Rob attempted to perform CPR on me and pushed his entire weight firmly into my ribcage. That squeezed the living daylights out of me and out popped my bewildered soul.

Expelled from my battered body, I found myself watching the scene from above as it unfolded in its whole macabre glory.

I saw myself on the ground, squashed under Rob's weight as he was vigorously punching my chest. His thrusts animated my body, forcing it into knee-jerk reactions. Every so often he would pinch my bleeding, runny nose and inflate me like a ball. Between gasps for air he would sob and scream, and whimper and urge me to get up. If there had ever been a chance of that happening, Rob had effectively managed to destroy it.

A man came running from the top of the road. He was breathless. 'I called an ambulance. It's on its way. I saw it happen. A car hit her. Hit and run … I got the numberplate!'

So that was it – I knew what had hit me, but it didn't make me feel any better. I was dead, or as good as, and the whole world had come to a standstill.

Life without me was unthinkable.

Only that morning I'd had it all well under control. My life was a well-oiled machine, ticking away like a Swiss clock, predictable. Every event – past and future – was scrupulously forecast and documented in my diary. I was smug in my custom-designed world. There were no surprises. I hated surprises. They threw me off.

The hit-and-run palaver threw me off big time.

That morning, as every morning, we had breakfast: cereal, semi-skimmed milk, tea. That was it. A healthy, no-nonsense breakfast which facilitated a self-restrained and consistent start to each day. I never varied breakfast, not on Sundays, not at Christmas, not on holidays. Breakfast was breakfast – a down-to-earth, regular routine. Anything over and above that would be sinful.

We ate in silence. We usually did. Emma was perched on the edge of her stool, half of her skinny backside sliding off it; one leg was propped on the rung of the stool, the other one outstretched, with toes pointing to the door – her typical 'on your marks' pose. She looked bored, which was normal for Emma. If anything was crossing her mind, she kept it to herself, under her unnaturally long and gothic black lashes. I often wondered how she managed to cultivate such long lashes, but never had the time to work it out. Or ask her. On the whole, we didn't say much to each other in our house, only the important things, like changes to our schedules or additions to the shopping list.

'I'm staying at Becky's tonight. Revising the Great Depression.'

'Get your change of clothes into the car. I'll drop you straight after school. I've got to go and see Grandma. Haven't been there since ... was it Tuesday last week?'

'She wouldn't know if it was Tuesday last year,' Mark shrugged.

'Finish your cereal!'

Under the veneer of sarcasm Mark was a big, floppy softy. He was still living with us at the less than tender age of twenty-three, his room an endearing mess of heavy metal posters, cheesy underwear, and law books. He was reading Law, just like his mother and father had. In his final year of university and flying higher than a kite on a breezy day, he had his life mapped out for him. He played cricket on Sundays, had a regular respectable girlfriend called Charlotte Palmer, spent most his evenings working, and was saving up to travel to the Far East on his gap year before finally taking up a post in one of the most prestigious city law firms. I was proud of him. He never gave us any trouble.

Mark looked like his father: tall and sinuous, long arms, long legs, a bit clunky in his unintended lengthiness. Obviously, as far as Rob went, that description would have fitted him twenty-five years ago. Now the long legs had become a bit spidery in appearance, the chest had caved somewhat and shoulders had dropped, but then that's what fifty years does to people if they don't keep fit. Rob didn't, and he was pushing fifty big time. He was an office mole. Thinning greying hair, glasses he polished with a clean white hankie every day at breakfast, Radio 2 crackling softly into his ear – he was no bother. I loved him the same way I had when we got married. It wasn't a passionate, carnal type of love. It was rather maternal: indulgent and tolerant. And there were only a few things I had to tolerate about Rob: the indecisiveness, the mumbling under his breath, the misplacing of things and, of course, the damned Radio 2 crackling away at breakfast time. Still, I loved him, which I often doubted was something he could say about me. He simply endured me, and on a good day was fond of me. Certainly not as fond as he was of Radio 2, though. Listening to Radio 2 was his major hobby. To be fair to him, he couldn't listen to me – I wasn't ever saying that much. I was busy.

'Off now!' I kissed him on the forehead. He glanced at me, puzzled, as if he was making every effort to remember who I was. I didn't have the time to wait for him to gather his wits and deliver a reply.

I was dropping Mark at uni first and then Emma at school. I did that every morning, always had. Rob would take a bus to work. That way he wouldn't have to trouble himself with the kids' school runs. And he liked reading on the bus, one thing you can't do when you're driving. His car, a comical Mini Cooper which only emphasised his awkward six-foot-plus frame when he sat in it, was tucked away in the garage, fresh as a daisy. Rob would take it out every two months to give it a wash and make sure the battery hadn't gone flat. It was a job he enjoyed – that, and feeding the cat. Every other job around the house was down to me, including school runs.

I drove on automatic pilot. I knew the steep, windy route up to Bristol University by heart. I blanked out the shenanigans of the morning traffic: the hysterical hooting, the fist-shaking, the killer looks. I ignored the suicidal pedestrians throwing themselves in front of the car, seemingly keen on certain and imminent death.

I didn't know then that I would be soon joining their ranks.

We weren't speaking. Emma and Mark sat at the back, looking away from each other. I liked having them in the car. They were safe with me. In two weeks' time Emma would be sweet sixteen. She acted twenty-nine and desperate. I didn't approve of the long lashes, short skirts, sheer tights, and push-up bras. Who was she trying to impress? It sent the wrong signals to any old pervert lurking out there. She was only a little girl. At her age I still rode my bicycle and wore socks with holes in them. Why couldn't she be more like me?

I kept asking her what she wanted to do with her life. She still didn't know if her usual 'Oh, leave off, Mum!' was anything to go by. Nevertheless, I shouldn't complain.

She was doing well at school and had recently taken to revising with Becky for their GCSEs. I liked Becky. She was plump, bland, and a straight-A student, if not particularly streetwise. A good, steady influence on Emma.

I had good kids. Nothing to worry about. I could take my eyes off them as much as I could take my eyes off the road, and think.

The morning drive was a perfect time for thinking. My mind wandered off to the Ehler case. I had been preparing for a lengthy, cut-throat trial – Tony always put up a decent fight for his clients – but, out of the blue, Ehler had pleaded guilty. Before sentencing, the judge would hear character witnesses and all that nauseating, sycophantic blabber about what an exemplary model of a son, husband, father, and citizen Michael Ehler happened to be. As far as I was concerned he was a small-time crook. Tony would, no doubt, try to get him off on a suspended custodial sentence and in no time his exemplary client would be back to rebuilding and selling stolen cars to supplement his modest panel beater's income. Over my dead body! I screamed inside. The time, manpower, effort, and money that went into catching those petty wheeler-dealers was enormous – the rewards mediocre. It was a Herculean task to make charges stick against them and I would be damned if I would let the cocky little bastard off the hook that easily!

I stopped at the usual spot, on a double yellow line, and let Mark out.

'Got some change for a sandwich?' He thanked me for the ride in his usual fashion and snatched a ten-pound note from my hand as if it was his due. I tried to calculate in my head how many sandwiches one could buy for a tenner a day, and how much of that money went towards that gap year in the Far East. Emma snorted at the back of the car. She was getting no cash for her sandwiches – the school cafeteria had a brilliant pre-paid card system in place.

As I arrived at court, I parked in a discreet corner and took out my make-up gear. By the time I finished applying deep crimson lipstick, heavy duty mascara, and glittering baby blue eyeshadow I looked like a common whore. I couldn't help it – I had to make myself desirable for Tony.

Tony pushed my buttons. All of them: the ones that made me go for his throat and fight him to death in court, and the naughty ones – ones that made me sweat oestrogen and dribble uncontrollably at the mere thought of him. I was a quivering teenager whenever he came close to me. He smelled good. There was something intoxicating about his scent. You wanted to lick it off him. Then there were those hands with the long, flat-tipped fingers, fingers that could play any woman like a church organ. He wore crisp white shirts with starched collars and cuffs. The silk rustled when he moved. His suits were tailor-made, hugging his toned body like a mould. You wanted to break that mould, tear it off him and let him take you there and then, in public view, against the wood-panelled wall or on the cold marble floor. You wanted the world to watch as he worked you with his organist's fingers and banged the living daylights out of you as you gasped for air without giving a toss about common sense.

I knew that ecstatic feeling only too well. It was only a year ago that our sordid affair had ended. It had started following a heated argument over my refusal to give his client a deal on a lesser charge. Forced by the judge to negotiate, we had been locked together in a room with a coffee maker and a plate of stale biscuits. I pointed my finger in his face, shouting, 'No! You'll listen! You'll listen to *me*, fuck you!'

He grabbed my hand and twisted it behind my back. His breath was on my face when he said, 'No, fuck *you*.' With his free hand he pulled up my skirt. It was a tight pencil skirt so I helped by wriggling my body for it to get over my hips. He ripped off my knickers and I undid his fly. In no time I was sitting on the conference table, knees up to my shoulders, my dagger-sharp high heels dangerously close to his face. He didn't even break sweat. His face remained impassive right through it. His body was cool. He smelled like a wild stag. I reeked of sex.

When we were finished, we told the judge we couldn't reach an agreement. We were back to square one. The trial went on for another two months and so did our sordid affair. We lived dangerously: in empty courtrooms with five minutes spare to the next hearing, in toilets, parking lots, and once in a hotel corridor before we could get to our room.

Tony had remained strangely detached. There was no emotion or tenderness to our encounters. I couldn't call them *lovemaking* as love didn't come into it. Sometimes I had the impression he didn't even like me, just wanted to fuck me and be done with it. The feeling was mutual. I didn't like Tony either, but that was of little importance. It was purely physical. We were like a pair of copulating rabbits: always in a hurry, fast, impatient, and then promptly on our separate ways. I took to wearing stockings and skimpy knickers with strategically placed slits to facilitate easy access and avoid tearing. We used no protection. For the thrills. The whole idea of fornication is to reproduce. We got off on the risk of that happening.

I wasn't proud of myself. I'm still not proud of myself. The best way to deal with it was to assign the whole episode to temporary madness. I had gone banging bonkers for a while and then it passed, and I was cured again. Cured and respectable. Except that I would still dress up and put on my whorish make-up when Tony was around, and I would wiggle my arse, performing my very own version of a mating ritual.

I checked myself in the rear view mirror. Good grief! I looked cheap. I despised myself. This explained why I couldn't bear Emma's elongated eyelashes and short skirts with those sodding sheer tights. I didn't want her to turn out the way I had. I wanted her to stay in control of her instincts. Respectability comes from self-restraint.

I got back into the saddle as soon as that trial was over. I lost. I hated losing; I had always been a bad loser. But in that case it was more than just losing the trial – it was the ultimate subjugation. Tony was on top of me, fucking me against my will. Professionally speaking. Professional rape. I ended the affair.

Of course, Tony thought I couldn't handle the defeat in court and this was my way of taking it out on him. But it wasn't about him. It was about me. I was losing my marbles. I had found myself staring down the barrel. If the madness was to go on, I would be consumed by it. My career would be over. I would lose my family. There would be chaos. I would be out of control. Rob would be free to go.

I loved Rob. He and I had a solid relationship. We had two beautiful children. We had order, purpose, and a good understanding. We were comfortable with each other to the extent that I could wee in the bathroom at the same time as he was cleaning his teeth. We could pass wind companionably while watching the news. And there was no madness. Not even when we first met.

It had been a fortuitous meeting, destiny in action from the word go. We met at the Edinburgh Festival. I was nineteen, in the first year of university. It was my first holiday away from my mother. She had held a powerful grip on me and my sister Paula, not to mention our long-suffering father. Mother had been a force to reckon with. Or to get away from, as far away as possible, as quickly as possible. My first step was to go backpacking with friends. Girlfriends. We romped around the Lake District, living on fresh air, cigarettes, and cheap wine. Some of us revelled in random sexual encounters with total strangers. Some of us, but not me. I was one of those prim and proper girls who was shit-scared of falling pregnant before her time. Plus I didn't hear the call that everyone else seemed to hear – the mating call. You could have diagnosed me as sexually retarded. I was waiting for Mr Right to come and deflower me on our wedding night. I had it all planned in my head.

We stopped over in Edinburgh for some 'cultural cleansing' before returning home to Bristol. The concert we went to would become the most significant milestone in my life. I can't remember the name of the band that played that night, but I recall blinding beams of light crossing above our heads and bouncing off our faces, turning us all into a broken collage of arms, torsos, heads, and grins, like a Cubist painting. I was wearing my ripped jeans and a cropped top with bare midriff – nothing spectacular. My girlfriends were long since lost in the crowd, probably copulating with random passers-by behind portaloos. I was sort of twitching to the music. A tall, lanky bloke appeared and started twitching next to me. I seized him in my peripheral vision: he was OK, a bit skinny, but then who wasn't at twenty-two? He had a punk hairdo and the long mild face of a little lamb. I gathered there was a reason to him dancing next to me, as in, he was about to chat me up. But he didn't. He didn't have the guts. I had to take the initiative and once I did, there was no going back.

Nodding my head to the music, I smiled at him. He responded.

'Do you like them?' he shouted over the noise.

'Yeah!' By then I was head-banging to show my appreciation.

'Me too.'

He was about to turn and walk away, when, panicked and desperate, I screeched alongside the lead singer, '*Uuuuhaaa!*'

He stopped and looked at me, intrigued. I felt like such a twat, but at least I had his attention. I performed an elaborate body twist – till then I didn't know I had it in me – and gave out another heartfelt '*Uuuuhaaa!*'

'Are you local?' I was keen to establish his credentials before going anywhere further with it.

'Bristol!'

'Nah, get out of here! Me too!'

He shook his head in disbelief.

'Working?'

'Studying!'

'I can't believe it! Me too! Don't tell me it's Bristol Uni?'

'It is!'

'You're kidding me!'

'Third year, Law!'

That was when I stopped twisting and twitching and stood dead in my tracks. I knew it then – it was *destiny*. 'First year, Law.' I said.

'What did you say?!'

'Take me out of here!'

'Where to?'

'Just somewhere else!'

We tumbled out into the streets of Edinburgh. I had no idea where I was, but I was in good, reliable hands.

'Got a name?' I asked him.

'Rob,' he said and fell silent. He was positively bewildered.

'I got a name, too. It's Georgiana.' And that dealt with all the preliminaries.

I was deflowered that very night in a dark alley, standing on an abandoned beer crate to match his height. The premature deflowering was the only thing that didn't go according to my plan, i.e. it didn't take place on our wedding night. But that was academic. I'd found my Mr Right – even if I had had to go all the way to Edinburgh to get him. From then on it was plain sailing. I had us engaged by Christmas and married two years later when I was three months pregnant with Mark. Mark was born two days after my graduation. Everything fell into place like tiny pieces of a puzzle. And I was the puzzle master; Rob was just watching, still very much bewildered – but happy, I led myself to believe.

I was happy too. Our family was my greatest achievement. I wasn't going to let a moment of madness destroy it. I ended it with Tony, reinstated myself in the driver's seat of life, and once again everything was fine and jolly, until the hit-and-run.

I am getting ahead of myself. Back to that fateful day …

It was going to be a long morning. There was a line-up of well-meaning relatives, friends, and neighbours willing to testify to Ehler's unassailable character. It was all but a formality, yet I was feeling restless. Something was niggling at the back of my mind. The guilty plea had come too easily. There was something to it. There had to be something to it. Tony didn't throw in the towel unless there was something bigger at stake. But what?

Jason Mahon, the juvenile in a stolen vehicle we had followed all the way to Ehler's garage, was yet to testify against him. He was jittery and highly unreliable, trapped into giving his testimony by a deal that would keep him out of prison but would destroy his budding criminal career. He could back out at any time. The connection between him and Ehler would be hard to establish. No one else was prepared to talk to us, and yet Ehler entered the guilty plea.

Of course, we had other evidence of cars with false papers and reinvented bodywork turning up on the market and a trail of crumbs leading to Ehler, but it was circumstantial. I had been looking forward to piecing it all together before the jury, exposing Ehler's trademark handiwork and blowing the network of his underage associates out of the water. His garage was the headquarters for small-time trade in stolen cars and he was the brains behind juvenile car crime in Clifton, where Jags and BMWs stood in every driveway – and where every well-connected resident had a high expectation of the law in action. The law had to be seen to be done.

I had already been relishing the sight of Tony's face as I dragged his client through the grilling cross-examination by my brilliant silk, Hugh Bramley-Jones, as I threw at him evidence he would have to sweat hard to repudiate, as the jury declared his client guilty, as the judge sent the bugger down. Defeating Tony would be orgasmic. I needed it. I had it all planned …

Then came the guilty plea. It felt as if someone – Tony – had pulled out my teeth. It just wasn't right. I had been deprived of the satisfaction of winning.

I sat through the excruciating catalogue of Ehler's good deeds and services to the community. Short of the young car thieves telling us what a star-of-the-year employer he was, we had heard from every Tom, Dick, and Harry. Tony was sprawled across the courtroom, smiling, looking relaxed. He definitely wasn't defeated. Quite the opposite, he was relieved.

'Could you please state your name, address, and occupation for the court,' the court clerk was initiating yet another character witness, an elderly man, stooped, shoddily dressed in an oversized, stained suit and striped tie straight from the seventies.

'Harold Prickwane, 24B Sparrow Rise, West Street, Bedminster … um, pensioner.'

Prickwane … Prickwane, what a funny name. I knew that name. That sort of ridiculous name always stuck …

As the old man was explaining his relationship to the accused as that of his father-in-law, I was frantically paging through my bundle of documents. I remembered that name from somewhere. It struck me as peculiar. I even remembered thinking that it wasn't a real name. Yes! I had it! *Prickwane Properties Limited!* That was the name of Ehler's landlord!

Ehler was allegedly a small fish who, upon reneging on his mortgage repayments and losing his house six years ago, earned himself an adverse credit rating and could no longer afford to own a property. The house he lived in, in the leafy area of Clifton, was rented. Poor chap had been – apparently – pushed into the life of crime by his financial difficulties. *To make ends meet,* as he himself had put it with a humble and plaintive expression in his face, *he would take on a dodgy car, without asking questions, repaint it, puff it up and pass it onto a dealer, make hardly any profit for his efforts ... That's all, your Highness ...* You almost felt for the poor bastard. Until now.

Ehler's landlord was Harold Prickwane, his father-in-law, who himself resided in a council flat in one of the shabbiest areas of Bristol! I scribbled a quick note to Hugh, saying: *He's Ehler's landlord. Prickwane Properties! Ask what he lives on.* Hugh obliged.

'Mr Prickwane, would you be so kind as to tell the Court what your monthly income is?'

'Me income?'

'What do you live on?'

'Me pension, what else?'

'How about the income from your properties?'

'Me what?' Harold Prickwane blinked. 'You trying to be funny or something?'

'My understanding is you're the director and sole shareholder of Prickwane Properties, a company that owns, amongst other properties, the house where your daughter and son-in-law live.'

'What's he on about?' Prickwane addressed the judge, who prompted him to answer the question.

'Let me help you there, Mr Prickwane, if you don't

mind my helping?'

Hugh was a brilliant Cheshire cat of a barrister. He was fat. He was smooth. And he was lethal. 'Perhaps you simply don't have the heart to charge rent to your own family. Is that it? Is that why you have to live on state support while being the proud owner of an estate worth over half a million pounds?'

'I owns Mick's house?' Harold Prickwane was laughing heartily. 'That's a good one, that is!' He was thoroughly amused, unlike Tony, who'd tensed up in his seat, looking pallid and seriously shaken. I had him! His silk raised an objection that Mr Prickwane was not on trial here. I didn't care. Hugh didn't care. We let the poor sod go. We had bigger fish to fry.

After the hearing, I phoned Tony to suggest lunch. I wanted to look him in the eye when I told him my plans for his client. I wanted to be sexy, predatory, deadly – everything he loved to fear in a woman. He agreed and I tarted myself up to the hilt: shedload of lipstick, buckets of *Opium*. God knows why (our sex-in-a-toilet-cubicle days were done and over with) but I shot out to Ann Summers and bought a pair of fishnets and crotchless knickers. Equipped for every possible climax, I headed to the Café Rouge.

I could feel goose pimples all over my body! This was the beginning of a long and tantalising battle. I knew in my bones that Ehler's panel-beating garage in Clifton was just the tip of an iceberg. There was more, much more to Mick Ehler than making ends meet!

Tony was waiting for me. He smiled, waved; I waved back and trotted to his table. I could smell his stag scent over my bucketfuls of *Opium*. Cold air tickled my naked groin. I felt drunk already. The large glass of red I'd ordered would see me under the table. I decided not to touch it.

'Congratulations,' Tony purred nonchalantly, 'you closed a case in under two weeks. It calls for a promotion. Director of Prosecutions? What do you think?'

'Not yet, Tony.'

'No? Family first, career second? It's not like you, Georgie.'

'I'm not talking about the promotion; I'll take it any time,' I purred back. 'It's the case that isn't over yet. I thought I should let you know –'

Our lunch arrived: my salad Nicoise, his risotto.

'So what is it you want to share with me? Something tasty, I hope?'

What a dirty tease, I thought, feeling sticky between my legs.

'Proceeds of Crime Act, Tony. You realise I can't let it go after this morning's revelations. I will be asking for full disclosure of your client's assets, bank accounts, directorships – the lot.'

'You'll be wasting your time and the taxpayer's money,' his voice was cold.

'Perhaps, but you know me – I'm a sucker for a challenge.' I laughed, but he didn't join me. 'I will be digging into the affairs of all of his relatives. Dead or alive. You never know what I may unearth.'

'A few corpses, I imagine.' This time he laughed. We clinked glasses mid-air. I decided to have my glass of red after all. Once again I was in control of myself and of events. I was looking forward to crossing swords with Tony and it looked like he was too.

I was late picking the girls up from the school gates. After my impromptu lunch with Tony, I had thrown myself into the frenzy of reconstructing Ehler's family tree: paternal, maternal, aunts and uncles, his wife's side inclusive. I cross-checked those names with Companies House. In no way was Harold Prickwane the mastermind – this much was certain. Prickwane was a dummy: a dumb dummy at that! The whole scheme was down to Ehler. Either he was running a lucrative money-laundering scam spread neatly amongst all his hapless relations, or I was The Queen of Sheba! And the question that begged an answer was this: where did the money come from if not from trade in stolen cars? Legitimate, hard-working panel beaters weren't generally self-made millionaires, with their tentacles hooked firmly into real estate and multiple travel agencies. And Ehler was, by proxy. The network of his family-based companies returning fat profits was elaborate. It had to – and I was sure it could – be traced back to Ehler. I called the Central Fraud Group to organise a meeting. I wanted them to start digging into it. This affair would see me rise to the top! My cheeks were burning and I could feel myself sweating with excitement, like a teenage girl with raging hormones. That was when I realised how late it was.

I shot across the city centre, merging onto countless roundabouts and flying under the white sails of Broadmead whilst cursing my dedication to work. I had got it from my father, I think, though I was never quite sure if he had been a genuine workaholic or simply lingered at work to avoid Mother at home. I leaned towards the latter.

As I languished at yet another red light, my mind was racing through the unthinkable: Emma there, on her own, outside the safety of the school grounds, in her sheer tights and short skirt, fluttering her long black lashes at the passing traffic ... She was only fifteen, for God's sake! I was twenty minutes late. Anything could happen in twenty minutes. Anything could happen in a split second! Becky had probably given up waiting and gone home by bus. My daughter was alone, alone against the legion of anonymous paedophiles this city was crawling with! Again, I started breaking out in a sweat. A cold sweat.

Then I saw them. Two girls – one short and chubby,

unattractive (oh, how I wished she was the one I had to watch over!), and the other one, the one I did have to worry about: tall, long-legged, unashamedly blonde, her bony hips pushed forward, her mannerisms provocative.

'Get in the car,' I hissed.

'You're late.'

'Hello, Mrs Ibsen!' The car wobbled comfortingly under Becky's weight.

I muttered a sulky greeting that was more like a growl than a spoken word. Nobody took any notice of my indicating so I braved it into the stream of traffic, hoping for a submissive driver. He was not that. It was a man in his late fifties, bald and furious-looking, driving a battered old Skoda, which lent itself to little or no respectability. He compensated by honking loudly and tailgating me all the way to the top of the road, where at last he turned and disappeared from my life forever.

The girls were texting each other at the back of the car. Their thumbs took turns to punctuate their mobile phones' screens. Maddening pings followed and explosions of conspiratorial laughter set my teeth on edge. I found it baffling how inept young people were these days at the art of face-to-face conversation. The spoken word was dead; dialogue subsisted only in foreign language classes. The youth of today were rude mutes with twitching thumbs and emoticons instead of faces.

'Noooo!' howled Becky after opening another message from my child.

'Yes!' my child countered. 'Do you want to see it?'

I saw a very keen nod in the rear view mirror.

'Promise to delete it straight away?'

Another nod.

Another maddening ping.

Another gasp for air and explosion of laughter.

'Delete it!'

'It's huge –'

'Shush! Mum ...'

'So when?'

Emma bit her lip and hit the touch screen of her phone. A few seconds later – Becky's phone's text alert, the sound of a slaughtered pig, resounded. She read the text and typed in a reply. Emma's phone screeched. She grinned, 'I'll be sixteen – I can do what I like.'

That was the longest sentence she had uttered in ages. It had put the fear of God in me. Alarm bells sounded in my head. What did mindless teenagers do when they turned sixteen these days? Got tattoos! Huge ones! What else? What else could be huge and forbidden at sixteen? A huge tattoo, or ... I couldn't contemplate any alternatives. Anyway, she wouldn't do anything like that. She was like me – or she was supposed to be – and I never did anything stupid. It had to be some ridiculous big tattoo. On her backside. Or her neck. She would regret it for the rest of her life. Over my dead body, I declared inwardly. Little did I know ...

I dropped them off in front of Becky's house. It was a reassuring red-brick end of terrace with a neat front garden brimming with lavender. An empty crisp packet was trapped in the bushes. I wished someone had picked it up, or preferably, that no one had dropped it there in the first place. Any sign of neglect attracted vandalism. Allowing litter in your front garden was serious neglect. How much did it take to pick up rubbish and put it away?

I was entertaining those dark thoughts as I was driving away. I stopped at the T-junction at the top of the road and glanced into my rear view mirror. A young man approached the girls, acting as if he knew them. He was scruffy, wearing a beanie and dirty, frayed joggers. I had the impression he knew the girls because he stood way too close to them. To be precise, he stood way too close to Emma. In fact, he and she leaned against each other, shoulder to shoulder. They laughed and their bodies parted. The young man shook his hand as if he'd been handling something very hot. Emma wagged her finger at him. He swerved and, briefly, I caught the glimpse of his face.

I knew him! He was Jason Mahon, my juvenile car thief from Ehler's case! The same square figure, the same thick black brows and large teeth. Becky pointed to my car and Jason squinted in my direction. I looked away, indicated to turn left. When I looked again, he was walking away, hands in the pockets of his joggers, head tucked between his shoulders. The girls had disappeared inside Becky's house.

There were several things I could've done, but didn't. I could have turned back, driven past the youth, taken a good look at him, even confronted him. I could've knocked on the door of Becky's house, asked about the young man and his relation to my daughter. But I didn't do any of it because it would have made me look foolish. Instead, I told myself not to be paranoid. I told myself it couldn't have been Jason; the world was full of scruffy young men dressed like hobos. They all looked alike.

As Jason Mahon's lookalike was sailing into the sunset, something was niggling at the back of my mind. Something about those two large front teeth sticking out and that narrow face of a weasel. Something about the way he hunched, burying his head between his shoulders. Something about the curious step that had the attitude of a swagger but the physicality of a limp, as if one leg was shorter than the other … I couldn't put my finger on it.

I cast my mind back to our numerous interviews when his lawyer and I haggled over a deal. I regretted now that we had reached an agreement; I didn't need young Jason any more now that Ehler had pleaded guilty. The little weasel didn't deserve a nice chummy arrangement allowing him to redirect his energies into a cosy apprenticeship of his own choosing. If I remembered correctly he had managed to secure a dishwasher's job in some restaurant. For how long would he stick to this new work experience before he returned to the life of crime? A dishwasher's pay would certainly inspire no loyalty.

What was it about those interviews that kept pushing Jason Mahon to the front of my mind?

Untypically of his age and profession he was rather outspoken. His account of Ehler's guilt was compelling.

'I knew Mr Ehler was after Jags. Vintage models, leather seats, wooden dashboard –'

'How did you know that?'

'Word gets out, innit?'

'Like?'

He gazed at me as if I were a halfwit. 'Like people got Jags and was told to get more of the same, if you know what I mean.'

'So Ehler would take any Jaguar off your hands?'

He nodded and spat through his teeth on the floor. It was bloody rude and he knew that, but he also knew that his testimony was more important to me than his manners.

'Did he pay well?'

'Cash on delivery. Always.'

'Always? It wasn't your first time then?'

Smelling a trap, he glanced quizzically into space.

'How many cars did you sell to Ehler?'

'Can't remember.'

'Try.'

'Can't. What's the point trying?'

'The point is you can land yourself in a sweet little cell where they have juicy fresh-faced eighteen-year-old dudes like you for breakfast. And then they pass them on ...'

'That's not necessary,' his sleepy lawyer intervened, feigning mild indignation, 'My client has already agreed to co-operate.'

25

'Lost count,' Jason said, spitting again.

'That many?'

'I didn't say *how many*.'

'Don't get smart, Jason, or we can terminate this interview here and now.'

He pushed his weasel's face forward towards me. I could see tiny thin hairs sprouting on his chin. He looked like a Kung Fu master. 'Mr Ehler buys every vintage you bring him, yeah? He got the demand, we got the supply. He gets them off our hands and one way or another resells them to the same arseholes we stole them from in the first place. My flatmate says is called wealth retribution, yeah?'

'*Redistribution*,' I corrected him mechanically, 'Wealth *redistribution*.'

'… is what I said, yeah? It's all business. No one gets hurt.'

'Right … So how many – roughly – has he bought from you for *redistribution?*'

'*Roughly* … eleven so far. But don't quote me on it cause I will deny it in your face, yeah?'

'That's not part of the deal,' his lawyer reminded him.

'Yeah, fuck it,' Jason conceded the point.

'You will have to come up with an employer's name, someone willing to take you on. It's a condition of your –'

'I got it, yeah? My flatmate got me a job in a joint where he works. They pay shit but it's a shit job so what d'you expect, yeah? Dishwasher.'

'Who is that flatmate of yours, Jason? I'm asking out of curiosity. He seems such a clever cookie …'

'He is. Smart, he is. A good mate of mine, yeah. He looks out for me.'

'Is he also involved with Ehler?'

'What you mean, "involved"?'

'Does he work for him?'

'Brandon?' Jason chuckled, genuinely amused. You never know what little things can make young delinquents happy nowadays. 'I told you Brandon's smart, didn't I?'

'You also told me he worked in some joint where the pay is shit. That doesn't make him particularly smart.'

'It don't make you smart 'cos you're a brief raking in shitloads of dosh, yeah? You still ask stupid questions, the lot of you. Told you, Brandon's smart – that's it.'

I chose to ignore the derogatory allusion to my profession's intellectual prowess. On some level I would have to agree with Jason: there were a few well-connected but intellectually handicapped employees of Crown Prosecutions who would struggle with the challenges of being a dishwasher. My understudy, Aitken, was one of them. He was in this job either because of his high-ranking relative or to fulfil some intellectual diversity quota or other. Still, stupidity could cast a long shadow and I didn't enjoy sitting in it, being verbally abused by failed teenage car thieves. So, pushing professional sensitivities aside, I proceeded with the interrogation.

'Does this Brandon of yours have a surname?'

'He must of!'

'OK. What is it then?'

'Dunno.'

'You share a flat with him and you don't know his name?'

'Why should I? He don't know mine. Anyways, he got no business with Ehler. Get my drift, lady?' There was a warning in Mahon's glare. I didn't want to lose his confidence (if I had it, that was).

'Fair enough … So you don't live with your parents, I take it?'

'My ma?' Jason chuckled again, but this time there was bitterness to the sound he made. 'You wouldn't risk living with her.'

'Why is that?'

'Just wouldn't. Trust me.'

'OK, I trust you. What is your address for the record,

Jason? Where can we find you?'

And that was where I suddenly remembered! The address Jason had given me! He'd said, '18 Gaolers Road.' I thought it pretty amusing: such an appropriate abode for a juvenile criminal. But that wasn't it! Gaolers Road was where Becky lived. Number 8. The young man displaying the highly disturbing familiarity with my daughter wasn't just Jason Mahon's lookalike. – He *was* Jason Mahon!

Mother was in the best care home money could buy. I visited her twice a week, or once at the very least. It was my duty to do so. Though she no longer knew who she was, I harboured an irrational fear that somewhere deep down in the recesses of her Swiss cheese brain, she was keeping a tally of my visits and before long would rise from her dementia like a phoenix from the ashes and hold me to account. Mother was a formidable presence in my life, even though my presence didn't register with her at all.

She was sitting in her comfy chair, propped up by several cushions. Her milky-brown stockings were twisted at her ankles, her cardigan collar up on one side and down on the other; the buttons were done up wrongly so that the last one had no buttonhole to go into. Mother's pale fingers were playing with that stray button, rubbing and pulling it mechanically. The radio was on, loud, but she wasn't listening to it. If I turned it off, however, she would become confused and might begin to cry. Her chair was by the window overlooking the park. Though she was facing that way, she wasn't looking. Her eyes were glazed over with incomprehension. If I pulled her away from that window, she would panic, would dig her fingernails into my arm and scream obscenities at me. I knew it because she had done that before. It was a revelation to learn she had such a colourful assembly of swear words.

As it was, she was at peace and perfectly indifferent to

me. Her bottom lip was quivering slightly; it looked as if she was talking to herself, ignoring me on purpose. I didn't take offence. She probably didn't mean to come across as inattentive. She probably didn't *mean* anything, but I had this distinct impression that whenever I came into her peripheral vision, she would become more animated: her bottom lip would quiver more emphatically and her fingers would pull and scratch at her buttons with greater gusto.

As always I sat on the edge of her bed, folded my arms and started telling her about everything that had happened in the past few days. I knew she liked detail; nothing to be withheld as too trivial, let her be the judge. Mother had always been attentive to detail. In the days when she knew who we all were, she had kept tabs on us. She knew everything and what she didn't know she expected us to tell her. So we did, usually at the dinner table, taking turns: Paula, Father, and I. Mother would listen and interrupt us unceremoniously with frequent reminders about our incompetence, stupidity, and limited prospects in life. I think it was her way of showing how much she cared about us.

It wasn't particularly graceful, but her criticism was the only way she could express her love for us. I felt it. Father and Paula probably did not. As I said before, Father avoided Mother. He was six years her junior and perhaps for that reason she often treated him like a child, chastising and telling him off, and generally putting him in his place. So he needed a safe haven: somewhere to hide and weather the storm. He found it in his work. He was the breadwinner, she was the homemaker. It had worked well for them for forty-five years of Father's active employment. Two years after retiring, he packed up and died. I had a sneaky suspicion that he had planned it all along. Sitting at home with Mother and her constant nattering didn't do much for his will to live.

Paula had done a runner, too. She was the wilder of the

two of us. Three years younger than me, she had always been the baby of the family, and Father's favourite. Mother didn't have favourites. We were equal failures in her eyes. I wasn't much affected by Mother's opinions; I guess, I understood where she was coming from – she wanted us to try harder and do better. Paula, on the other hand, took everything to heart. At eighteen she left home for good to study drama; she went to London, as far away from home as possible. It was as if she had run away with the circus. We hardly heard from her, not even birthday cards. She had turned up for my wedding with a black boyfriend, giving Mother a near-seizure. She then abandoned the boyfriend halfway through the evening and started flirting shamelessly with Rob, giving *me* a near-seizure. It was sobering – the moment they first set eyes on each other she went for him like a vulture for dead meat; he acted the part to perfection. It was so undignified, even to watch – a grown man unable to tell the cow to fuck off! I almost felt sorry for him.

I was glad to see the back of her when she left at dawn. For me, she was a lost cause already then. I didn't want to know her. I crossed her off my Christmas card list. She was as good as dead to me, and I rejoiced.

Mother, on the other hand, had found Paula's second disappearing act difficult to swallow. I think she waited for her to come back, for many years. She kept saying Paula would return, but Paula never did, leaving me to fill the hole in Mother's heart and patch up the one in mine. I had the upper hand. I was the good child. I stayed close to my parents, especially Mother. I had to please her. I had to weed out every last memory of Paula. Banish the cow to hell.

I followed the right path. I became who Mother had secretly aspired for me to become, even though she would never dare say it out loud: a strong, successful professional blessed with a happy family, respectable husband, and a big house in the best part of town. The only thing I couldn't be was a man. I knew Mother would've liked that very, very much. She considered it a personal tragedy that both Paula and I were girls. She had toughened us up from an early age, but that would never compensate for the lack of what she most craved for us to possess – a penis.

At least she had one male figure in her life: Father. Despite her regular chiding she loved him deeply. She clung on to him for dear life. He validated her. When he died suddenly of a stroke, two years into retirement, Mother's dementia had kicked in. She didn't want to know anything any more so she took it all out of her mind. I am afraid that included me. I was a stranger to her, a speck of dust on the perfectly clean and smooth surface of her mind – I just bounced off it.

Our family photograph stood by her bedside. It had been taken thirty years ago, before our lives splintered in all possible directions, before Paula escaped, before I got married and had my own children to take me on my own path to dementia. Unwittingly, Mother had thrown a used handkerchief over the photo, obscuring everyone who was in it. I picked up the hankie and wiped the dust from the picture with it. I couldn't help myself. For the first time I noticed that no one in that photo was smiling. We were all posing with a gravity that reflected the general tone of our family life. I passed the hankie to Mother. She blew her nose into it and pushed it nervously under the sleeve of her cardigan, like a hamster.

'Disposable tissues are much more hygienic,' I said without a hope of Mother taking any notice of me.

After relaying to her the latest developments in Ehler's case, I squeezed her hand and kissed her on the forehead, neither of which she acknowledged.

'I'll be going then. See you next week, Mum. Keep warm, the nights are still cold.' I was heading for the door, expecting nothing from her. There she surprised me. I

31

heard her say with lucidity that astounded me, 'Should you be wearing a skirt above your knee? At your age?'

For a split second I saw the old, familiar expression of severe condemnation in her eyes, and it made me feel warm inside.

Rob had arrived home before me. He was in the garden when I got there. He was kneeling on the ground; his back was arched like a humping greyhound's. He was stabbing the soil with a fork, eradicating weeds. Defeated dandelion leaves lay on a sacrificial pyre behind him. He knew I was home because I flung the window open and kicked the cat out. The cat scampered past him, jumped onto the fence and from there glared at me resentfully. Rob ignored both of us.

I threw the dinner into the oven: grilled chicken and chips. I was working on the assumption that Mark would be turning up for dinner. If he didn't, the cat would have the chicken and the chips would go to the pigs (if we had any). I hated wasting food, but I refused to abandon the hope that my boy would join us for dinner. Since the kids gained independence, Rob and I had lost the pleasure of their company. Most days it was just the two of us staring at each other silently over the salad bowl.

I had just enough time to go for a run. It was my escape. Rob tended to the garden, I tended to my muscle mass. I would run religiously every day before dinner unless there was a snow blizzard or a torrential downpour. That day we had lovely weather. The air was calm and still, smelling of lavender. I changed into my tracksuit.

My mobile rang.

'Mum, hold the dinner off, will you?'

'What time will you be here?'

'Give us an hour.'

'Us?'

'Charlotte's coming.'

'Next time it'd be nice if you told me in advance.'

'I am telling you in advance.'

He sounded as if he was doing me a favour. Perhaps he was. He could've gone to Charlotte's for dinner, sat down at a table with Charlotte's parents, chatted and bonded with them instead of us. I should be grateful.

I turned off the oven. When I came back from running, I would have to add more chips and another piece of chicken. The salad bowl would need to be shared amongst four but, lo and behold, it might even witness some table conversation!

I smiled to my reflection in the mirror as I was pulling my hair into a tight ponytail and admiring my altogether rather tight body. History was repeating itself, I thought. Charlotte was a law student, in the same year as Mark. She had a razor-sharp mind and the determined strength of an ox. She reminded me of me. And Mark was just like his dad.

'Out for a run!' I shouted to Rob and the cat on the fence. Rob rose from his knees, wiped his trousers and waved to me, heading in as I was heading out. Sometimes I wondered if he waited for me to leave before coming back inside for a cuppa. The cat was coming back indoors too, doing his best to trip Rob up on his way.

I slammed the door and ran into the front garden. There was a piece of crumpled up litter on our driveway. It must have travelled from the neighbours'. I picked it up fastidiously and chucked it into the neighbours' wheelie bin, which was already out for tomorrow's collection. Then I stepped into the road, heard a screech of tyres, and that was when it hit me.

FULL DISCLOSURE ...

The doctor spoke with an accent, rolling his Rs heavily and emphasising words that didn't matter. He articulated them slowly as if it was Rob who was a foreigner with poor grasp of English. Perhaps Rob needed that. There was a wild look in his eyes, a look of fanatical disbelief. He was still clutching the kettle, now with both his hands as if it was an urn holding my freshly processed ashes. I doubt he realised that he was wearing no shoes, just socks, and the left sock sported a hole over his big toe. He must've left his muddy boots in the garden. Although considering the state of his boots (no laces, soles coming off, and the forlorn smell and look of something fished out of a sewer) the bare socks were probably less embarrassing after all.

'I AM Dr Jarzecki. Please TAKE a seat, Mr Ibsen.'

The command seemed like the most sensible induction into what would follow next.

'Oh, yes! A seat!' Rob enthused. He went around in circles like a dog chasing its tail, found two chairs, sat in one, placed the kettle on the other one, lifted one leg over the other, peered with horror at his left toe, hid both feet under the chair, then picked up the kettle from the neighbouring seat and held it defensively in his lap. 'Is she going to be all right?'

'She eez in a critical CONdition. She suffered eg-stensive injuries to DA head and chest. Several brocken reebs, da collar bon ... cardiac ARRest. She eezn't out of da danger ZON. Not by far.'

Both Rob and I focussed all our powers of comprehension on the good doctor's lips. It was a bit like watching one of those Swedish crime series where something went wrong with subtitles and you have to try to lip-read and fall back on your common sense and imagination to follow the plot.

'So she'll be all right?'

The good doctor stared, clearly baffled by Rob's conclusion. Then he started again, only slower and louder, 'Her heart stopped for MANY minutes. Da scan shows DIP fractures to her skull and seVEre swelling in her brain. Interior bleeding. She eez in an inDUCED coma, Mr Ibsen. We deed all we could, but you must PREpare for da vorst …'

The subtitles were not back yet and it took Rob a while to catch up with Dr Jarzecki.

'What are you saying?'

'Der eez always hop, but your wife MY not make eet, I AM very sorry. We are doing what we can, but … What I am saying eez, BE prepared for da vorst.'

'Can I see her, please?'

Rob dragged the kettle to my room with him. He put it on the bedside table as if it was a vase of flowers. Having dealt with the kettle, he disintegrated into a plastic chair that stood next to my bed. His whole back caved in as if, suddenly, someone had pulled his spine out of it. He stretched his arm out to take my hand, but upon seeing all the plasters, tubes and needles stuck into it, pulled back, only his fingertips touching mine. His body shook with a sob.

I wished I could hug him and make him stop. If only he knew I was still around, and kicking! Indeed, I tried to kick him but I didn't seem to be in possession of any feet. I attempted to blow into his face – if I were a ghost, I should be able to generate some paranormal activities! Knocking. Whispering in the dark. Forcing the kettle to fly off the bedside table … Nothing worked. I obviously wasn't a fully-fledged ghost. In simple terms I was neither hither nor thither. It was a strange state of affairs. You could say my inner lining had detached from my outer body. You could say my soul was born, the umbilical cord severed and I – the spiritual I – was free to romp. As far as I could see there was no dependency on the mother ship which was my material form, though I dreaded to think what would happen if the mother ship went into permanent shutdown. A coma was the best compromise I could hope for under the circumstances.

Rob went on sobbing and I could do nothing about it. I must agree with him that I was a sorry sight. My head was bandaged, my face swollen and discoloured. It looked misshapen, like a potato. My body was laden. I too felt like crying.

'Dad?'

Mark was standing in the doorway, looking aghast. There was a hint of accusation in his tone. It was aimed at Rob, as if he knew that his father's botched CPR had sent me on my merry way into eternity.

Rob rose from the plastic chair and rushed to hold Mark. He needed holding, too. They stood there in each other's arms for a while.

'What happened?' Charlotte's voice came from behind Mark. 'Your neighbour told us there was an accident.'

'Hit and run.' Rob pulled away from Mark and withdrew to his plastic chair. 'She is in a coma.'

'She'll be all right, right?'

'Of course, she'll be all right!' Charlotte knew something nobody else did. 'Medicine today does miracles.'

Mark, my poor Mark, wasn't quite up to standing. I could see his legs were failing him. He staggered and collapsed on the end of my bed. He was pale and could easily pass for a ghost even though I was supposed to be the ghost here, if not a fully qualified one. He didn't dare look at my bruised face as if looking would cement the fact of my dying – make it irreversible. Seeing me there would be an acknowledgement of that fact for when you see things you don't believe in you're forced to start believing.

Like his father earlier, Mark reached for my hand. He squeezed it. 'Mum?' Briefly, his eyes travelled to my face; he gasped and looked away, but his hand stayed locked on mine.

The hardest thing about the out-of-body experience is that you can't feel. I couldn't feel my son touching my hand and I couldn't conjure that feeling up from the past either – the last time Mark had held my hand was when he was a toddler. After that, he refused.

'She can't hear you, she's in a coma.'

'Of course she can,' Charlotte was quick to contradict Rob. 'People in a coma can hear you, it's a proven fact.' She was such a know-it-all, but it *was* a fact: I could hear them. 'Talk to her, squeeze her hand ... Mrs Ibsen!' she raised her voice at me as if I was an old dear with a hearing aid out of batteries. 'Mrs Ibsen, it's me, Charlotte! Mark is here too, sitting on your bed, holding your hand. Can you feel it? You'll be all right! Go on, Mark, squeeze her hand!'

Instead of doing as he was told, Mark stared at her, bewildered. Rob did too. For some reason, he had picked his kettle off the bedside table and was clutching on to it.

'Oh, the kettle! The kettle is here! We were wondering about the kettle. We found the front door wide open, thought there was a burglary. Mark went upstairs with his cricket bat. I checked downstairs, went to the kitchen, found the kettle missing ... Strange, I thought, that they would steal a kettle in this day and age ... I knew something was seriously wrong when I saw Mrs Ibsen's mobile phone on the kitchen table. A burglar would've taken that rather than the silly kettle. Mark came down, said everything seemed OK. I told him about the kettle. We were beginning to worry, like, really worry, when Rowan from next door turned up. She told us ... We rushed here straight away. We borrowed your car, if that's OK?'

Rob was still staring at her. Charlotte was a big girl. I don't mean she was fat, just tall, big bones, wide chest, that sort of big. She had that poster girl look, like Anna Kournikova. It seemed as if Rob was seeing her for the first time in his life – he was analysing her physique with great concentration.

'Yes, that's fine,' he mumbled after a long, attentive pause.

'Have you eaten?'

'Eaten?'

'No, I don't think so.'

'You must be hungry? Mark, are you hungry?'

'Hungry?' Mark and Rob kept repeating after her as if they were learning a new language.

'Wait here!' She turned on her heel and disappeared.

I like Charlotte, but I must admit I was relieved to see her go. She had taken over the entire Intensive Care ward, sidelined me, talked over me, just marginalised me all together. What a character!

When she left, Rob replied to Mark's earlier question.

'We must prepare ourselves for the worst.'

Mark started crying.

It was nice and quiet for a while, the three of us sitting together in silence. There was no rush. I was in no rush. They just sat with me. I watched them: they were like two peas in a pod, father and son. As long as they were here in this room with me, they would be fine, but outside …

That was when I started to worry. Rob was no survivor, and Mark was just like him. He had Charlotte and she would be his mainstay, but Rob? He would have to do the school runs, remember things, make decisions … He would have to step outside his garden and off the bus, into the real world. The kids would go astray. Bills would be unpaid. Electricity would be cut off. The house would be

41

repossessed. No one would visit Mother. She would be livid!

I really had to get over this, I told myself. Concentrate on coming back from the dead.

'Hello again!' Charlotte reappeared, carrying three pizza boxes and a bottle of Coca-Cola. 'You need some refreshments: can't starve yourselves to death! I didn't know your favourite, Mr Ibsen. I got you ham and cheese, to be on the safe side. Mark, you have your finger-licking-good BBQ chicken!'

Rob capped his face in his hands and rocked in his plastic chair. He looked like a schizophrenic who had just heard those dreadful voices telling him to kill someone. I guess that someone was Charlotte. Mark looked equally traumatised. 'Charlotte, we're not hungry. NOT HUNGRY!'

'You don't realise how hungry you are!'

'Go home, Char, please, go home!'

'But –'

'Take my car,' Rob offered. 'We'll be staying here a bit longer. Take my car. And go,' he smiled at her apologetically. 'And thanks for … everything.'

Charlotte bit her lip, picked up the pizza boxes, and marched out of the room. I saw her throw the boxes into the rubbish bin before she whizzed off in Rob's car. Till then I didn't know she could waste food like that. I didn't know she was such a little madam either.

There was no point rattling about the hospital corridors. My two men were fast asleep. Rob was snoring softly in his plastic chair, his head thrown back and mouth wide open, nursing in his lap the now indispensable kettle. Mark was lying face down on the far end of my bed, his legs hanging off, his feet dangling comically. Two nurses were chatting casually about me and the man in a neighbouring room; one was betting on me kicking the bucket first, the other one's bet was on the man. He was on his fifth heart attack, a no-hoper. Sure enough, an alarm rang from the man's bedside and both nurses dived in to save him. Doctor Jarzecki turned up instantly and began shouting orders in his theatrically rrrolled-Rs accent. It seemed to me that the nurse whose bet was on the man wasn't really giving her best to deliver him from the jaws of death. Maybe her heart wasn't in it, considering that her mind was already made up. She was right. Two minutes into the resuscitation the man's spirit left the room and bumped into me in the corridor. He gave me an almighty fright.

'I've had it,' he said. 'I'm off.'

'Hi.' I felt a bit idiotic talking to a ghost, but it would be rude to pretend I didn't see him. We were in the same boat, though technically he was already overboard and I was still clinging on. 'I'm next door. Um ... nice to meet you. Sorry to see you ... go.'

He was a short-tempered man. 'Bah! Don't worry, no one else is. They've had enough of my antics! Frankly, so have I. Fifth heart attack in so many years! Pain in the arse! Oh well, clearly I'm needed in higher places.'

He floated away with a purposeful whoosh. Only at that point did I look about me and realised that the place was full of people just like me and him: some of us hanging on to our earthly remains, others strolling boldly into their tunnels of light. I wasn't ready to join their ranks. I had things to do, things that couldn't be done from the relative safety of heaven. Anyway, I thought with a shudder, there were no guarantees I'd be going to heaven and not the other way. I'd stick around if it was all the same to God. He probably didn't have much use for me up there at the moment, considering that all my responsibilities were down here. Emma was one of them.

It was quite a revelation to realise that I wasn't bound to my body. I could leave it behind and it wouldn't miss

43

me. There was no place I couldn't be and I didn't have to travel to get there. All I had to do was to focus on the person I wanted to be with, and presto, I would find myself by their side, as if teleported, but without the excess luggage of my earthly body. In fact, I could probably be in two places at the same time. In three, four, twenty places! I was omnipresent, not unlike God Himself. Now that I had proof that He could exist, I really had to start taking Him seriously. Just in case.

It was a bright morning: clear skies, trees in the park bursting with pollen, buses bursting with fumes. It was the rush hour. People went about their business of commuting to work and begrudging God for it.

I found Emma sitting on the bus, next to Becky. This time they were communicating without the aid of their mobile phones. There was lots of giggling, nudging, and 'Oh, my God, you *didn't*, did you?' Unlike her usual apathetic self, Emma was positively excited. Her cheeks were glowing pink. Her voice was loud.

There was a brief moment when I felt deeply resentful: here she was having a whale of a good time while her mother – *me!* – was lying there on her deathbed. Then I realised she didn't know. No one had told her. After the long night's vigil, Rob and Mark were fast asleep by my side. They had forgotten Emma. I shook with frustration. Rob! I knew he wouldn't cope. I knew he would forget to pay the bills and put the rubbish out, but it didn't occur to me he would forget he had a daughter!

'He said he'd get fresh sheets, brand new from the shop.'

'Did he? Why would he?'

'Don't you know?' Emma gazed at Becky, incredulous. 'Because everything has to be perfect for my first time. The sheets will be clean. And white. You know?'

Becky shook her head.

'Like a bride's dress. Isn't that cute?'

My ears pricked. *First time for what? Bride's dress?*
Did I dare to speculate what my fifteen-year-old daughter
was talking about? God, no! I had been such an idiot! All
mothers are. Never letting our little baby girls grow up.
Fussing around with ribbons and white socks while our
little bundles of joy conspire to turn us into grandmothers
at the first opportunity ... So no, that huge thing on the
phone hadn't been a tattoo! Where was my daughter going
with it? And where was her father? Where was Rob?

'You sure you gonna go through with it?'

'I love him, Becky.'

'I see ...'

'He loves me.'

'How do you know?' *Becky, that's just what I wanted
to ask!*

'I know it. I just do. I know it in my gut. You know?
Down there,' Emma put her hand on her lower abdomen.
'I know it in every part of my body.'

'Ah! I wish ...' Becky gazed at her dreamily. Then she
sobered up, 'But what if you get ... you know?
Pregnant ...'

'I won't. We'll use a condom.'

My heart sank. It was a distinctly physical sensation
within my strictly ghostly form. How come I hadn't see it
coming? Never mind Rob, where had *I* been in the last five
years? I expected my family to be immaculately virginal
on every level. I expected no deviation from the picture
perfect I had in my mind. What was I thinking! They were
only human, but I was hardly ever there to get to know
them. What I knew about them was sweet fuck all! I
should've been angry with myself, but I don't have it in
me to take the blame. So I blamed that ... that ... that
lecherous dickhead! It was his fault! Oh, how I raged! My
daughter's future was being trampled over by some dirty
old bastard and I couldn't do anything to stop him! I
couldn't burst onto the scene and strangle him with my

45

own bare hands. I couldn't get Rob to do it (though I doubt he would be up to it even if he knew what was going on). I couldn't call the police. My hands were tied by my incapacity. More than that! I was not in command of my own hands! All due to a freaky, random hit-and-run! The timing of it could not have been any more inconvenient!

The girls were laughing, looking at the screen of Emma's mobile.

'Show me the other one!' Becky implored.

'Which other one?'

'You know which one!'

A nudge, a wink, a giggle. Emma touched the screen. Their heads hung over it as Becky gasped with a 'Wow!' and Emma laughed. I could see what it was: a photograph of a naked torso. Emma flicked her fingers over it and zoomed in on the part of the photo that displayed something misshapen and unsightly, something the colour of a worm, one with a swollen head and one eye. Something that could only be summed up as an erect penis.

Good Lord!

I stared in horror. Was there no end to the man's depravity?

Emma slid her finger across the screen and another picture came into focus. The nasty paedophile surprised me. He wasn't as old, fat, bald, and slimy as I had imagined. For one thing, he was young and slim. And he had hair.

'He looks like Jamie Oliver. It's like … weird that he's a chef, you know?' Becky offered me another piece of intelligence.

A chef? A dishwasher more likely. Good grief!

'He's a palaeontologist, actually. He told me last night. I always knew there was more to him than al pesto.'

'Palaeontologist!' Becky and I exclaimed at the same time. Becky added, 'Is that like … dinosaurs? How cool is that!'

'He couldn't find a job.'

Why am I not surprised!

'But he likes being a chef.'

And he likes innocent fifteen-year-old girls! Someone call the police!

'You're so lucky, Em!'

Emma glanced back at Becky in that condescending way only she could. 'Luck has nothing to do with it. You have to go and get it. Veni, vidi, vici!'

'What?'

'I liked him the moment I saw him, and I always get what I like.' She shrugged.

'You do? So what's that got to do with Da Vinci?' Becky was trying to get her head around the Latin.

'Never mind that, it's something I heard … Probably from Mum. It's like, "you go get it, girl", yeah? So I did. I had to lie about my age at first, but that's all behind us. And now he's all mine.'

I hated to admit it, but she was more like me than I could ever imagine. She had it all mapped out in her head, even though, I feared, it was a road to hell. But she was my flesh and blood, she was me – and at that moment, I knew nothing would stop her. Little minx!

Emma jumped as her mobile rang in her hand. She put it to her ear. 'Dad? What is it? What …' The colour drained from her face. The smile had vanished. 'She'll be all right, right?' Mark had asked the same question, so I knew what Rob's answer would be. Emma was bravely holding back tears and trying to sound mature.

'Which hospital? I must see her. I've no money for a bus fare, Mum was picking me up after school … can you pick me up? Now? Please?'

Her hands were shaking as she lowered the phone into her lap and looked at Becky with disbelief.

'It's my mum …'

47

It's funny how even in a near-death situation we tend to stick to our daily routines. Straight from 'dropping off' Emma by my hospital bed, I headed for the office. I was conscious of the meeting I had arranged with someone called Ridley from the CPS's Central Fraud Group. I had to have the investigation into Ehler's affairs started before I could ask for an adjournment in sentencing. At this late stage the judge would frown on adding new charges. And I would have to explain myself to my superiors. Extra expenses in a case that was cut and dried and on the verge of a successful conclusion would not go down well. I would have to show solid prospects for success. I knew I could, but even though I was there in spirit, the *in body* part was sadly missing. And that complicated matters somewhat.

When I saw that pimply twit Aitken sprawled at my desk, I knew there was no hope. The smug grin on his face signified nothing but the intoxication of power, with no room for conscious thought. Related to some posh public servant holding high office in London, Aitken was on a fast-track ride to the top. He would spare neither the time nor the attention to the messy job of pulling the guts out of my cut-and-dried case. He would sew up the corpse nice and quick, and claim the credit for it. No doubt would enter his small mind unless he saw a greater benefit in it for himself.

I crossed my fingers – the virtual ones – and urged him by my sheer willpower to look into my notes. Ehler's fat file was lying in front of him, unopened. The frayed green ribbon was tied up as I had left it the previous day. The printouts from Companies House were inside. Even if he saw them, would he have the brains to make the connection between the long line of Prickwanes with multiple investments and one small-time panel beater who had fallen on hard times in this bad world of ours? Would he have the curiosity to investigate the links?

He wouldn't.

Aitken was sipping coffee from an extra-large Starbucks mug. He picked up the phone.

'Ali, what's in Georgie's diary for today? Uh-huh … OK, slow down a bit! Got that …'

He was taking notes on his mobile phone. He was entering my diary dates into his calendar! He was taking over my job, the twat! And I wasn't even cold in my grave yet!

'No, no, it's fine! I can manage. We don't need to put anything off. Thanks. Oh, one more thing! Can you get IT to unblock Georgie's account? I want to check her emails. Just to stay on top of things till she comes back.' '*If* she comes back', he mouthed under his breath. 'Good girl, thank you.'

He leaned back in *my* chair and stretched his legs under *my* desk; stared at the ceiling and smiled; wiggled, displeased. He looked for the lever under the seat, found it and began re-adjusting the chair to his height. He returned to the chair, and smiled again. I wished I could wipe that stupid pompous grin off his pimply face.

Ali rang and confirmed he could now access my computer. He thanked her and called her, again, a 'good girl'. My blood boiled. Ali was at least twenty years his senior!

Still, there he was, on my computer.

Perhaps there was hope after all, I thought. Perhaps he would check my notes on Ehler's case. I'd left a trail of Companies House searches and a draft brief for the guy from CFG. But Aitken the Twat wasn't looking at case notes. Firstly, he went into my emails and scanned for any personal ones. There weren't any. I have a private Hotmail account. He didn't bother opening a single one of my work emails. My fingers were itching to do that for him. There was one from CFG, hopefully confirming today's appointment.

Aitken abandoned my email account and moved to my internet history. One by one, he ventured into every single website I had looked at in the past, including the singles dating site I had joined a few months ago out of boredom or stupidity, or both. I couldn't explain why I had gone there and what I had been looking for. Maybe an antidote to the haunting memories of my hot romps with Tony …

Aitken was relishing his finds. His grin was getting wider.

The telephone beeped.

'Yes, Ali?' Aitken scowled. Quickly he glanced at his electronic diary. 'There's nothing in her diary about that … hmm … well, OK, send him in.'

A man in black with a military bounce in his stride walked in.

'Thomas Ridley, CFG.'

'Gavin Aitken.'

'I'm sorry to hear about Mrs Ibsen's accident.'

'We're all shocked.' Aitken pointed to a chair and the man in black sat down.

'You're OK for a drink?'

'Coffee'd be nice.'

The pimply twit phoned through to Ali with the order.

'This meeting,' he started hesitantly, 'wasn't in Georgie's … Mrs Ibsen's diary …'

'She only telephoned yesterday to arrange it. She felt it was urgent as the case had already reached the sentencing stage.'

'And which case is that?'

'Michael Ehler. Receiving stolen property, I understand. I see from my briefing she felt there were grounds for money laundering charges. At least a possibility –'

'Oh, that!' Aitken butted in with the knowing expression of someone who actually had a clue. He didn't. 'No, no … I looked at Ehler's case closely. Only this morning. It's cut and dried, but there's nothing more to it. Georgie could be … sometimes … well … over-diligent.'

They both smiled.

'I see,' said the man in black.

'It would be a waste of taxpayers' money if we pursued it any further. It's a dead end. Ehler is a small fish. That was a one-off, actually. One of those unfortunate chaps the recession hit harder than others. Thoroughly honest otherwise. Clean record, clean as a whistle …'

'I see,' the man in black repeated.

'Sentencing today. I won't be asking for a custodial sentence. It wouldn't serve any purpose. Wouldn't serve the public interest in any shape or form. The man is of better use working in his shop and paying his taxes.'

'Then it was a waste of time coming here.' The man in black stood up.

'Sorry about that.'

Ali walked in with the coffee as they were shaking hands, bidding each other a good day in a chummy sort of fashion.

'We won't need that coffee after all, Ali,' Aitken declared imperiously.

I could've strangled him in all his sanctimonious smugness.

Tony was in court long before the sentencing was to start. Clearly he wanted to talk. He wanted to talk me out of pursuing his panel-beating client. He was surprised to see the pompous pimply twat instead of me. At first he was surprised, then his brain began to tick. I could tell he didn't know about my accident, but he was glad to be faced with a new adversary. A much less formidable adversary. A much less experienced one. An idiot.

Tony dashed out towards Aitken with his arms wide open. He patted him on the back, asked after his posh uncle in London, chatted about his summer plans. Ibiza was indeed the place to be this summer!

'The judge won't like the idea of adjournment,' Tony pointed out casually after the long preliminaries aimed at weakening his opponent's resistance. 'With only two weeks to summer break … well, judges are only human. They too have deadlines to meet. They too like their cases done and dusted before –'

'We won't be asking for an adjournment,' Aitken was glowing in his momentary glory.

'You won't?'

'I decided it wouldn't be in the public interest.'

'*You* decided? I can't say I don't agree, but does Georgie?'

'You don't know? You don't know what happened?'

'Well, I was wondering why you –'

Aitken interrupted. He clearly didn't like the slightest intimation that he was only a stand-in, a second-best. 'I took over Georgie's cases on top of my own. While she is convalescing.'

'Has she been taken ill?' I could see relief spilling across Tony's face like liquid honey. He must have considered himself the luckiest man on this planet.

'No, not ill. She was run over by a car. Hit and run. She's in a coma. Critical, I'm afraid.'

Tony's face had undergone a sudden transformation. The smirk of sweet relief was gone. He went tangibly pale. For a second I thought he would faint, but he only sat down. I sat there with him. Minutes passed in stony silence. I wished I could kiss him. He was seriously shaken. I hadn't dared to think he actually cared about me. But he did. He cared more than I had imagined.

To say that I was flattered would be an understatement. I was touched to the core.

Tony sat through the hearing and went through the motions with an absent look in his eyes. He nodded curtly as Ehler thanked him for his efforts. Ehler himself was beaming like a newborn baby with a silver spoon between his teeth. That didn't surprise me – the devil had got away with murder! A suspended sentence was a joke.

Aitken, too, was immensely pleased with himself. He was on a high, filled with adoration for himself which no one else seemed to share.

Bramley-Jones looked at him in sheer frustration. 'As long as you're absolutely sure, Gavin.'

'The case is closed. It may not be a concern for you, but I am accountable for every penny spent and the cost of grasping at straws is way too high in this economic climate.'

'If you say so. Georgie, however –'

'It's out of Georgie's hands.'

'So it is.'

If Bramley-Jones had any temper, he held it back well. I, on the other hand, was fuming. As soon as I was out of this flipping coma, I would bite Aitken's head off and serve it to the wolves on a golden platter. I didn't care how influential his relatives were. I just wanted his blood. Arrogant little prig! An idiot. All he was fit for was to stack shelves at a supermarket.

I couldn't bear being around him. Neither could Bramley-Jones. He took himself away from the pimply twat. Walking down the steps, he caught up with Tony.

'Congratulations are in order!'

'Thank you,' was the dry response.

'If Georgie were here –'

'I know.'

'I can't believe what happened to her.'

To that there was no reply. Tony buckled under his words. He looked beaten up. Sick.

Bramley-Jones gazed into his eyes, alarmed. 'Are you all right, my man?'

'Yes. Yes, thank you,' Tony sounded as if he was

pulling himself out of a slippery well. Every word seemed a superhuman effort. 'I must go. Sorry.'

I was drained. Life without me teemed with emotions. It was too much to handle. I needed a break: to sit somewhere quietly with a cup of tea and a Kit Kat. I guess in my earthly life that would mean a lunch break. Since in the spirit world food and beverages weren't on the cards – and neither was idle sitting – I went to see Mother.

It appeared that, since I saw her yesterday, she had not moved from her chair by the window. Neither had she changed her clothes. There was a cup of milky tea and some Rich Tea biscuits by her side, ready to be had any time this century. Mother wasn't in a hurry. These days, haste didn't touch the surface of her existence.

I thought I would just sit with her and keep her company. Together, we would companionably blank out the world. After all, nowadays, we had much more in common than we had ever had: we were both in a semi-vegetative state, teetering between living and dying, not quite able to make up our minds. She was muttering under her breath, her lower lip quivering as usual. My eyes followed hers into the park outside the window. The lawns were mowed and manicured to clinical perfection; hedges were sculpted into the shape of truncated prisms which resembled coffins. Mother was looking beyond them, into a copse.

There was a look of great concentration on her face, the sort children have when they learn a new trick, like using a knife and fork. When I glanced up into the biggest tree in the copse I could see why she was so focused. Mother was climbing the tree.

It wasn't Mother as she was now; it was Mother when she had been about seven. She was a bright-eyed and bushy-tailed tomboy, wearing a pair of high-waisted shorts on elasticised braces and a straw hat. There were five rascals about her age swarming around the tree, all boys apart from Mother. She was taller and more agile than them. Her bare feet clung to the tree like a snail. She was balancing on the sloping trunk which hung over a bubbling brook, letting its branches down to tease the current. She was pulling herself up, higher than the others, always ahead of the pack.

'Grab that branch! Not that one! That one!' She was guiding a boy with two front teeth missing. He strained and wobbled on his toes, but couldn't reach the branch. His face dropped into a scowl.

'Here, give me your hand. I'll pull you.'

She was hanging upside down, her legs hooked on a branch, her arms stretched towards the boy. Their hands met as he leapt up, but he was too heavy for her. Slowly his fingers slipped from her grasp and he plummeted into the brook, screaming his head off as he bounced off the lower hanging branches. The others gasped as they were splashed with water. Seeing his fall from the tree (and from grace), and fearing his potential drowning, my seven-year-old mother unhooked her legs and dived head first into the stream. Even though I had the obvious hindsight knowledge that she must have made it safely to the bank, I froze. No need: within seconds both the boy's head and hers bobbed on the surface. They were both laughing and spitting water – a loud, hysterical surge of heightened adrenalin. As they waded over to the bank, Mother poured water out of her straw hat and stuck it back on her head. Long, dark green weed curled around the brim like a snake. Her shorts were swelling with water.

Paula turned up from nowhere in her usual Paula fashion. She was all glamour and no substance. One look at her crimson cheeks and stage makeup and I began to wonder if she had only just left the set of *Macbeth*. Her face was frozen in an expression of permanent shock. I couldn't tell if it was Paula in character or in Botox. She was skin and bone: Pilates and egg whites taken to a new level of self-obliteration. She produced a bunch of grapes and a flamboyant bouquet, potentially recycled from her latest premiere. Her hands were claw-like and the black nail varnish didn't help to dispel the impression she had just stepped out of her grave.

She dug one of her claws into Rob's shoulder. 'And I was always the accident-prone one in the family,' she intoned dramatically. Paula had a way of making a dramatic entrance. She made Rob jump. He stared at her, clearly not having the faintest idea who the apparition was.

She sat on my bed and crossed her legs. Her heels alone could kill. Rob watched her, fascinated. Or frightened. He fidgeted, looking for something to comfort him. The kettle would have come in handy, but it was no longer on my bedside table. I wondered if it had got home at last, or if someone had stolen it. It was a decent kettle. I gave it to Rob two years ago, for his forty-fifth birthday.

'I came as soon as I heard. Luckily, I'm friends with Tony Sebastian. We frequent the same places. Old friends. He told me.' How the hell did she know Tony? His and Paula's social circles weren't exactly a Venn diagram!

Were they?

Rob shook his head, indicating he was lost.

'Tony, Tony Sebastian,' Paula cocked her head, 'he knows Georgiana *quite* well, I understand … They're … hmm … *friends*. Surely, you've heard of him?'

I didn't like Paula's tone. It was incriminating. How much did she know, the dirty old coquette? She'd never stopped being a troublemaker, and wouldn't pass up the opportunity to undermine my marriage, ever since the wedding night, come to think about it. Would Tony have told her about us …?

'Yes, I know Tony Sebastian. Vaguely …'

'Small world!'

'I'm sorry, forgive me, but it's you ... I don't know who *you* are.'

She was gobsmacked. 'Ah! You don't remember me. Have I changed that much? It's the shock, I'm sure.' She uncrossed her legs *Basic Instinct*-esque and followed Rob's downward spiralling gaze with an indulgent smirk, clearly hoping that the inside of her thighs would refresh his memory much quicker than her face. 'Let me take you down memory lane, shall I, Rob darling? Last time we saw each other was at your wedding. We shared a few drinks. A few too many,' she laughed. 'It's ancient history, really ... Now, let me think ... We go back even further: a chilly New Year's Eve party, star-studded sky, ground frost that could *penetrate* one right up to one's –'

'I'm sorry ... I didn't recognise you. It's Paula, isn't it?' Rob was pale, his complexion blending well with the colour of my deathbed sheets.

'Paula! Paula, but of course! Ten out of ten!' She was laughing even louder now. The whole hospital could hear her; even the dead had arisen. 'Georgiana's little sister Paula!'

'Sorry, Paula, so sorry, I didn't recognise you,' Rob repeated in a desperate attempt to shut her up.

'Oh, darling, I'll have to forgive you.' She patted his knee, her bony fingers stretching towards his groin. 'Under the circumstances you can be excused for being a tiny bit forgetful ...' She gave me a throwaway glance. 'So, how is she?'

Paula took Rob out of the 'stuffy hospital' for coffee and a chat at La Rochelle. It was her favourite spot, she said. She had been back in Bristol for five years now, performing at the Hippodrome, did Rob know? But then how would he? No one would've told him; she kept a low profile. Given their past, she didn't want to intrude on his marital bliss. Georgie wouldn't understand. *Like hell, I wouldn't!* I still didn't. I couldn't make heads or tails of the link between them. Considering that we had Paula in the equation, it had to be something seriously unholy. And what was it about the star-studded sky on New Year's Eve? Which New Year's Eve? She had been out of town for over twenty years! And what unthinkable filth exactly had passed between Paula and my husband when she accosted him at our wedding, and he rolled over and played dead for her entertainment? I could never quite take that image out of my mind: a cat toying around with a dead mouse, just for the heck of it. I vaguely recalled seeing her steamroll out of the men's toilet, the hem of her red dress just about covering her then still-perky arse. I still remembered wondering what the fuck she was doing in the men's toilet ... Getting lost in her drunken stupor? Or getting laid? I would never know, but I was wary of her now that she'd suddenly decided to set foot on my patch.

My darling sister Paula posed a threat to the sanity and stability of my family, which was particularly unnerving because, as it happened, I wasn't around to defend myself, or them. She had the floor, and she seemed to have my husband by the balls. She blathered on like a scratchy old vinyl record, over the hum of the restaurant, over my thoughts, over Rob's head. She had thought of visiting us but all she had managed was to visit Mother a couple of times. It was such a traumatic experience! Mother wasn't who she used to be. Paula felt Mother didn't welcome her visits so she stopped bothering the old dear.

They ordered: Rob took tea and a piece of cake; Paula managed a glass of water. She was full, she said. Full of shit, said I. They didn't talk about me. I might as well have been dead and buried for years – old news, yesterday's snow ... It was all about Paula. She was 'between relationships'.

'And content with it, darling Rob,' she chirped. 'Relationships are so high-maintenance! And men just take. Rarely do they give anything back. I give all I have. I give myself unconditionally. You, of all people, should know … So, in the long run, you see, it isn't fair on me.'

Stiff as stiff could be, Rob nodded. Did he know what she was talking about? I sure as hell didn't. No one took anything from Paula. It was the other way around. Paula had always been a taker. Was I a taker too? Was he making comparisons between us? Was he petrified of what similarities he saw between me and that sore excuse of a sister with whom I had the misfortune of sharing a gene or two?

Paula smiled at him plaintively. I couldn't say if she was being nostalgic about her past or seizing her new conquest. She watched Rob eat his cake. There was satisfaction in her eyes as if she was having the cake with him – anorexics usually compensate by vicarious eating, or talking excessively about food. 'I don't mind the coffee cake. Is it good?'

Rob nodded.

'Sometimes it isn't their best offering. Too dry for me. My favourite – and they don't seem to have it today or I'd be devouring it, believe me! – my favourite is New York cheesecake. That creamy, rich vanilla topping over a simple biscuit base does it for me, darling Rob.' She was obviously quoting a recipe, for the real thing had never passed her lips.

'I like it, too,' Rob confessed.

'No!' she laughed. 'I knew you were a cheesecake lad! You and I …' She indulged in a sip of mineral water and peered at Rob greedily from under her false lashes. I didn't know if it was Rob or his cake she was after. Probably both, but Rob, carrying less calories, had to be her first choice.

You call that a sister, I snorted inwardly.

'I was a tiny little bit hurt when you didn't recognise me.'

Paula was sitting, cross-legged for the time being, in my lounge. She had invited herself into my house and was helping herself to my wine even though Rob was firmly under the impression that he was the driving force behind it. She had even made him share the bottle with her. 'It helps you put things into perspective, Rob darling,' she assured him.

Rob was a poor drinker. A couple of sips and he was all yours. *Or hers*?

She swooped around the room, touching ornaments and family mementos with her grubby claws and smiling with an indulgent, smug spark in her eye as if they were all her memories. She talked incessantly about her glam career and tragic love life. She threw in a few spicy details here and there for effect – to arouse Rob. What man wouldn't harden ever so slightly upon hearing about the size and firmness of her nipples when she forgot her bra at her first audition for *Educating Rita*? And the onstage chemistry between her and her partner was so sizzling that each time they acted out intimacy she could feel his hard-on against her thighs? She couldn't help but part her thighs for him.

'Acting is just being yourself in front of other people – in other words: living your life on stage,' she mused.

Halfway through the bottle, Rob was pickled with a hard-on of his own hidden under his cupped hands and Paula was back on the sofa, all over him like a nettle rash.

'I so get into character, body and soul. It becomes reality for me, better than the real thing.' She stretched, thrusting the daggers of her jutting collar bones at him. She was purring by now, drunk on her own eloquence. 'I draw on my own life experiences, when I'm on stage. It all becomes blurred: life, the stage, life again … In *Educating Rita* I drew on that night when you and I … so young, so hungry … Do you know how old I was? Not sixteen yet.'

Rob swallowed hard. *What was she on about?* Fantasist, I had to remind myself, pinch myself on my ethereal arm.

And yet, why was Rob looking so sheepish?

'I should thank you for it. My Rita was a flying success. You remember what a cold night it was, don't you?'

Rob could not bring himself to deny that he did. His silence spoke volumes. It was less trouble because if he spoke whatever he would say could be used in evidence against him. So he sat there, mum and mystic like a sphinx weathering the sand storm, waiting for Paula to stop. But Paula would not be stopped. She was up and going. Letting the sleeping *bitch* lie was out of the question. I was beside myself – no! not just this comatose beside myself, but the good and proper beside-myself-with-anger!

'There was chemistry between us, I could feel it. Could you?'

Luckily for Rob, the bell rang. He excused himself and rushed for the safety of our front door. Paula growled, baring her canines. For her own sake, I was glad she didn't get a chance to bare any other part of her anatomy.

It was the police: Detective Sergeant Thackeray with a sidekick. I vaguely knew Thackeray. He was a decent man, very straight and thorough. A bit right-wing, but that was what made him a good policeman. He had a thick neck and a round, bald head, giving him a bullish appearance.

Rob had led him to the lounge, where Thackeray gazed critically at the heavily made-up woman in high heels and with an alcoholic beverage in her hand. His gaze travelled to my husband, who coughed guiltily and introduced the witch as 'my wife's sister'.

'Yes,' Thackeray muttered doubtfully.

'Miss Paula Smythe,' the witch announced imperiously and offered her hand for Thackeray to kiss.

He took it and shook it awkwardly. 'Yes. DS Thackeray. How is Mrs Ibsen?' he asked Rob.

'No change. She's in a coma.'

'I'm sorry.'

Rob's partial hard-on had worn off and he was able to offer Thackeray a seat. Paula wondered if the detective 'would care for a glass of wine?'

'No, thank you, ma'am.' He didn't look at her when he answered, forcing himself to be polite. 'We have some information, Mr Ibsen. We found the car that was used in the hit-and-run. It was abandoned only two streets away from here. A vintage Aston Martin. Quite rare, as you may imagine. It wasn't hard to track down the owner. He had reported the car stolen only minutes before the incident. Fortunately for us there's CCTV footage. We have an image of the thief …'

Thackeray's constable passed a picture to Rob. 'Do you know this man? Have you seen him before?'

'Is he the one who …'

'Yes. Do you know who he is?'

'No, never met him.'

Paula peered over Rob's shoulder. 'Quite young … The hit-and-run – opportunistic, would you say? Joyrider?'

'We're not so sure, ma'am. He took the car, drove straight to this house, and then abandoned it immediately afterwards.'

'He was in shock. Just killed someone … I too would drop the bloody knife with which I just killed someone …' She would! She would drop the knife and wash her hands and tell the bloody spot to go away. And if it didn't, she would go straight for the best stain removing product money could buy. Lady Macbeth could learn a thing or two from Paula.

'Or perhaps his purpose was achieved and he didn't need the car any more?' Thackeray mused aloud.

'You're not suggesting he intended to –' Rob gasped.

'We can't exclude any possibility, sir. He disarmed a sophisticated alarm. Not every Tom, Dick, and Harry can

do that. We will find this man. It's a small community –
car thieves.'

Paula resumed the chase as soon as Thackeray and his
constable stepped out the door. Her legs parted, once again
a faithful replica of Sharon Stone in *Basic Instinct*. Rob
obliged with a furtive glance up her thighs.

'Should we have some more wine?' she raised her
empty glass.

'Dad? Was that the police?'

The intimacy took an instant flight out of the window
and Paula's knobbly knees clanked together. None of us
had realised Emma was home. Rob flushed beetroot red.

'When did you come home?'

'Didn't go anywhere. Gave school a miss. How's
Mum?' Emma glared at the witch. The question that she
was really asking was, who the hell is *that*?

'No change. We have to be patient.'

'And who the hell is that?'

'Emma, watch your language … please.'

'Emma, darling, how you've grown!' Paula lavished
my daughter with theatrical affection. What a
performance! Worthy of a BAFTA! The bloody cow had
never even met Emma. I'd bet, until now, she hadn't even
known Emma existed.

'This is your Aunt Paula. Mum's sister.'

'Mum's *younger* sister. Come, give us a hug!'

Emma ducked the embrace and looked the creature up
and down. She wasn't taken by her aunt's ebullient
manner, nor was she impressed by her firm nipples. 'Good
timing,' she said. 'Mum's down and Aunty turns up out of
the blue. Is she moving in with us?'

'Of course not. She's visiting. Try to be civil.'

Paula's feathers were seriously ruffled. 'She's certainly
inherited Georgiana's pleasant attitude,' she snorted.

Emma ignored her and asked her father, 'What did the

police have to say?'

'They've got the man's picture. From a CCTV camera. They'll catch him.'

Emma sniffed Paula's empty glass. 'Mum won't be impressed.'

'What's got into you, Emma?'

She didn't deem it fit to reply. She opened the fridge, picked out a few slices of ham, and ate them with her fingers; drank milk straight from the bottle and walked away without as much as a glance back at her mortified father and disgruntled aunt. *My girl*!

'Where are you going?'

'Back to my room. Things to do. Tomorrow, I want to go with you to see Mum. I take it you're going.'

Rob turned to Paula, looking apologetic. 'I don't know what got into her. The accident –'

'Threw her off, I'm sure. Georgiana would be proud of her if she could see her now,' Paula chose to be magnanimous in her venomous sort of way. Enduring the family reunion thing with some panache, she added, 'It was nice to meet her at last. Any other offspring lurking in the broom cupboard?'

Mark wasn't in the broom cupboard – he was with me, in the hospital. Charlotte stood agitated by his side. She gave a few heavy sighs and went on biting her cuticles. Mark paid no attention to her antics.

'I don't want to sound insensitive, but there's little you can do here.'

A nurse walked in. If two women could be the polar opposites of each other, that nurse and Charlotte were exactly that. The nurse was a tiny elfish creature, small and delicate, her complexion dark, her eyes oriental in shape and colour. Her vulnerability contrasted with Charlotte's Nordic athleticism. Mark watched her as she collected data from the instruments I was attached to, and made notes on my chart. Charlotte took out her mobile and started flicking through screens.

'Mobile telephones are not allowed. Please switch it off,' the little nurse said in an equally little, twinkling voice which, surprisingly, came across as final and authoritative.

'They always say that,' Charlotte attempted to play down the warning, speaking over the nurse without looking at her, 'but it makes no difference.'

'Or leave the ward if you wish to make emergency calls,' the stubborn little nurse said.

'Surely –'

'Turn it off,' Mark told Charlotte.

'For God's sake, Mark!' Charlotte threw her phone into her bag.

The nurse drew the curtain around my bed. 'It is the washing time,' she said. 'You may want to take a break.' Unlike Dr Jarzecki, the nurse's Rs failed to resonate; she couldn't pronounce them at all. She sounded like Pontius Pilate in *Monty Python's Life of Brian*.

'Hallelujah! We really have to pick up the ring.' Charlotte took possession of Mark's arm and dragged him out of my room. They stopped outside the window that allowed a view of my room. Through a gap in the curtain you could see the nurse pull the sheets from my legs. My feet looked ghostly white. The sight caught Mark's eye. He winced.

'You go. I'll stay a while longer.'

'Don't you think we should be there together to pick it up? It's my engagement ring! Or have you changed your mind.'

'Your timing is a bit off, don't *you* think?'

Tears welled up in poor Charlotte's eyes. I was beginning to feel sorry for her. It wasn't her fault some joyriding bastard decided to knock me over at the worst possible time. Announcing your engagement over your mother's deathbed may be a bit of a stretch, but I could see how keen she was. Frankly, I didn't mind if they both went and collected the ring. I would have however appreciated it if next time – if there *was* a next time – I was given advance notice.

Mark was watching the little nurse through the gap in the curtain. She was small but strong; she rolled my lifeless body from side to side effortlessly to change the sheets and apply cream to my back and buttocks. It wasn't the most dignifying experience for me to have my backside exposed to the world, but in all fairness Mark wasn't looking at my bottom. He was looking at the nurse's. It was a tight, round bum, filling her uniform to the brim as she bent over my bed to puff up my pillow.

Naughty!

The nurse caught him. She glanced back and fixed him with an icy glare. Mark turned rapidly and looked behind him as if someone was there, someone he held solely responsible for this compromising situation. The nurse's face lifted in a pretty little smile. There was definitely something about her which made you want to take care of her. Meantime, she was rather competently taking care of me – while Mark drooled over her behind.

She finished, put my hands on top of the sheets and opened the curtains. She was such a fast and no-nonsense professional that she reminded me of an ant. Come to think about it, her body was also shaped in the likeness of an ant: tiny waist, round behind, round face with high cheekbones and almond-shaped eyes (I don't know why but I always believed ants had almond-shaped eyes).

'She'll be all right, right?' Mark was standing behind her.

The little ant-nurse peered at him and didn't smile. 'I don't know. People survive worse ... I would ask Dr Jarzecki.'

'I'm asking you.'

'I hope.'

'Just hope?'

'I am not a doctor, sorry.'

'So very little hope, then?'

The almond-shaped eyes rounded as she looked straight back at him. She clearly wouldn't lie. 'I must go,' she said.

'I'm Mark. Could you tell me your name? Please.' He caught her wrist to stop her going. Soon we would have the security on our backs and my son would be marched off the premises in shame for molesting the staff.

'Chi.'

'Chi?'

'It's Vietnamese. I really have to go.' She didn't try to pull away from him.

'You smell of hope.' I didn't realise Mark had it in him to be so profound.

She smiled. The little white pearls of her teeth looked almost unreal. 'I smell of hospital.'

'That's hope, I guess.'

'Other patients are waiting.'

'Don't be offended, please, but if I let you go, can I see you when you finish? I'll wait.'

Chi tilted her head and gazed at my son earnestly. She wasn't offended but neither was she sure she could trust him. Even I didn't know what he was playing at, and I was his mother!

'Please.'

'My shift has only just started. It's a night shift. I think you should go home, have a good night's sleep.'

'I think so, too. I'll be here in the morning.'

Mark found Rob sprawled on the sofa in the lounge. His head was pushed awkwardly against the arm of the sofa. It looked as if he had a broken neck. His body was stripped to his underwear and it was twisted in such a way that his left arm was wrapped around his waist and his right foot was propped against the floor, preventing him from rolling down.

'Dad?' Mark leaned over him to check if his old man was still alive. He smelled alcohol on his breath. 'Dad, for God's sake, get up and go to bed! You stink!'

'He can't,' Emma came out from the kitchen with another few slices of ham. Obviously Rob had embarked on a project of starving the kids to death and drinking himself into an early grave. 'He can't, 'cause there's a loose woman in Mum and Dad's bedroom.'

Rob mumbled something undecipherable under his smelly breath and turned, pushing his face into the back of the sofa.

'He's got a woman in the bedroom?'

'The official version is that she's our aunt.'

'Do we have an aunt?'

'Now we do.'

'Aunty Paula. My wife's sister,' a voice said from the back of the sofa.

In his room, Mark deleted three text messages from Charlotte without reading them. He then turned off his mobile, something he had clearly never done before because he had to play with different buttons to work out which one was the power-off one.

He flung open the window and switched off the lights. I could hear him fiddling with paper; rolling a joint. He lit it, and inhaled. The flame from the match illuminated his face briefly. He lay on his bed without taking off his shoes. As he exhaled, a thin shadow of smoke rose to the ceiling. All I could see was the glimmering end of the joint as my healthy-living, sensible son dragged on it. Weed wasn't something I would ever put him next to. What next? Crack dens and whorehouses?

Or Vietnamese nurses?

Where was Charlotte when you needed her? I resented her sensitivity and her stupid, girly sulkiness. She didn't know how to keep a man. She had no staying power, silly child!

'Chi ... Chi ... Chi ...' Mark was telling himself, testing the word, experimenting with it. He was clearly revelling in it. 'Chi ... Chi ...'

His room, as his mind, was full of smoke, stink and filth. My son was in a downward spiral.

I fled down to the lounge and curled up on the sofa, next to my unconscious husband. I didn't feel like contemplating the speed with which every sense and sensibility took leave of my family. My daughter was engaging in underage sex, my son was a drug addict, and my husband had succumbed to alcoholism. I couldn't face it. All I could and wanted to do was to lie next to Rob and feed off his bodily warmth, even though his bodily scent left a lot to be desired. He was breathing steadily, with an occasional snort and a grunt, and a dribble of saliva on his chin. He was in a deep slumber, flat on his back, his legs and his arms spread wide. He was wearing his boxers with the Tasmanian Devil print. Chic and so endearing! I kissed him and tried to take my mind off things. Sleeping wasn't something I could do and the state of constant consciousness was proving unbearable. I wished I could close my eyes.

I saw her float down the stairs like a bloody ghost. I say *bloody* not only because she set my teeth on edge but also because she was wearing red lingerie, the colour of fresh blood. Her hair was down, long to her waist. The high heels were off and her calves had lost some of their definition, and she was still painfully skinny, not an ounce of fat on her over-exercised flat stomach, with its muscles straining under the paper-thin skin like some alien foetus.

Paula, my whorish little sister, knelt by my sleeping

husband and slid her claws up his hairy legs towards those Tasmanian Devil boxers. Her fingers disappeared briefly under the fabric. Rob groaned and turned on the sofa. I could see he was grinning stupidly in his no doubt *wet* dream.

Paula drew her fingertips across his flabby stomach, leant over him, and licked – yes! LICKED! – his earlobe. She whispered, 'Robby, darling, come upstairs …'

It was the first time in my life that I was grateful to Rob for farting. He passed wind, rather loudly. It was a jolly small explosion. Wine never did any good to his stomach. He smiled beatifically and the magic was gone.

Paula scowled and scampered back to the bedroom. I swore revenge.

No one apart from Emma bothered to get out of bed in the morning. The place stank of alcohol and weed. Two empty wine bottles lay on the floor. One was dripping red wine, which was soaking into my carpet. I would never get it out.

I had to get out of there to keep my sanity intact. I followed Emma to school.

Well, I thought she was going to school, but I was wrong. She took a bus to Gaolers Road. She strolled by Becky's house as if she'd never heard of her and headed directly for number 18.

Jason Mahon's den.

So there I was, following my child into the jaws of depravity and danger, unable to stop her. Voyeurism had never been my way of dealing with life, but what choice did I have other than to watch?

The front door wasn't locked: clearly, there was nothing worth stealing inside. Emma pushed it open. It was an old house from the turn of the last century, with now-stylish bay windows on the outside and rot on the inside. The wallpaper on the walls used to be a stripy green but it had faded to a faint vomit-coloured stain. Someone had taken with their nails to stripping it off, but he or she gave up halfway through the exercise. Raised voices travelled from the direction of the kitchen.

'Shit! Shit! Shit!'

'Why did you do it? What the fuck did you think would happen?'

'You told me –' Sobs drowned the rest of the words.

'*I* told you? You've got the nerve! You fucking arsehole!'

'You told me to see things through to the end, yeah! "*Don't give up, Jason. Follow your dreams, Jason. Go and get it, Jason. The world is your bloody oyster!*" Look where you got me! Fuck you!'

'Well, fuck you! I was helping you get your priorities straight, man! I was helping you get out of a hole, you fuckwit! And you go and get yourself into a deeper one!'

'Shit, what do I do?'

'Now? What can you do now? It's too late. You can't undo it. Pray.'

'You not fucking serious! I know her, fuck! She knows me! What if she –'

'All right?' Emma was standing in the door.

Jason Weasel Face Mahon pushed by her and charged out of the room with a parting, 'Fuck!'

'Em!' The young man from Emma's mobile phone, the one with the lean torso and erect penis, smiled at her and came up to kiss her. His blond Jamie Oliver tresses were longer and greasier than in the photo.

'What's wrong with Jason?'

'Got a girl into trouble, I'm afraid.'

'Oh?'

'I don't think he'd like it if I talked about it. It's a bit of a fuck-up. Anyway, let's not waste time on Jason and his girlies. You don't want to be one of them?'

'God no!' Emma laughed.

'Good.' They kissed. A long, wet, tonsil-probing kiss. On me, it had the effect of sharp nails scratching glass. Thankfully, Emma pulled away and collapsed on a dirty settee, next to a gaping hole with a broken spring and a selection of empty chocolate and crisps wrappers. I half expected to find used condoms and discarded syringes in there too so I averted my eyes.

'Drink?' asked the poster boy and headed for the fridge. I feared I would see a bottle of super-strong cider emerging from there, but to my relief I discovered neatly labelled shelves, each with the name of its resident owner, laden with such wholesome goodness as celery sticks, cheese, and skimmed milk. I saw five shelves with five different labels – at least five different tenants shared this establishment. Hopefully, a decent proportion of them were not car thieves.

The poster boy passed a glass of milk to my offspring. 'So what's with school today?'

'Didn't feel like it.'

'I don't like it, Em.'

'I think I'm entitled, you know! Mum's accident … Then, yesterday, Dad brings home this woman, says she's my aunt. They get drunk. Dad never drinks.'

'I'm sorry, Em.'

He sat next to her and put his arm around her. She rested her head on his shoulder, closed her eyes. 'What's going on, Brandon? It's like a bad dream. I'm hoping to wake up from it, and I can't!'

'It'll pass. Accidents happen. Shit happens. People get over it.'

Words of wisdom! My shock and my anger were wearing off. At least Emma had someone to lean on, I thought. He wouldn't be my first choice of a shoulder to cry on, but he was there for her. A palaeontologist trying his hand at cooking, I mused, sounded respectable enough.

72

It sounded much better than an unemployed bum. But what was his association with Jason Mahon?

'I was going to see the *Lord of the Rings* marathon. It's starting in the Watershed in about half an hour. Want to come?'

Lord of the Rings? I pricked up my ears. Was Brandon – the poster-boy sex god – a closet hobbit? I was beginning to see him in a different light. I could almost spot the luxuriant hairs sprouting over his feet. Those feet were large enough. And the content of his fridge spoke volumes of his natural partiality to good wholesome food. Right, I concluded, this here hobbit posed no real danger to my daughter. I was leaning towards humouring him for the time being.

I left Emma and Brandon in a half-empty cinema, sharing a bag of popcorn in seats F7 and F8. I chose to overlook the fact that his hand was on my daughter's knee. Considering the fact that she was wearing tight jeans it would be a tall order for him to get into her knickers on this occasion. Anyway, I rested assured they were planning the Big Bang on her sixteenth birthday, by which time I was hoping to be back on my feet to put a stop to it.

Meantime, I had a horny witch on the loose in my house, hovering dangerously close to my hapless husband. I had to keep an eye on her. I expected the worst. I could only expect the worst from Paula. Any minute now she would spread her wings – or her legs. She could only tease with subtle innuendos for a short while. After that she would let it rip: full-blown and unprotected revelations. She and Rob … What hold did she have over him? What was there between them? I still hoped it was all only in her dirty mind, but for how long would it stay there, and there alone?

And that was the problem – Paula lived for the moment. She was bound to put her theories to the test, and

73

she would persevere on her seduction trail until Rob finally capitulated. She would devour him if he wasn't careful. I had no illusions about her. I knew her like I knew myself. I had to count on Rob, but right now I didn't fancy my chances.

I found her leaving my house in a strop. Rob had already disappeared with his tail between his legs. He probably had a serious hangover, and a few doubts about a wet patch inside his boxers. He left no forwarding address for Paula, no note inviting her to make herself at home. It had been a silent retreat.

Paula wouldn't be seen dead taking a bus. Public transport didn't go with red lingerie and ten-inch heels. Neither did walking. She helped herself to Rob's Mini. It stalled twice before it started and then it went huffing, puffing, stuttering, and screeching while Paula man-handled the gear stick and cursed like a trooper. She was only forty-two but her eyes were bloodshot and underlined with black rings and running mascara. Her skin was crumpled. She looked old, which provided me with some consolation.

I was curious to explore her life 'between relationships', but to my surprise she drove to see Mother. The carers had never seen her before in the Home and didn't believe her when she said she was the daughter. They knew my mother's daughter – they knew me. Paula couldn't have come from the same mother's womb. Still, she bulldozed her way in and accosted Mother in the same place and position I had left her the day before. The Rich Tea biscuit was untouched; the milky tea corpse-cold.

'Now, now, Mummy, don't tell me *you* don't remember me!' Paula peered into Mother's vacant eyes. There was nothing in them, let alone joy. Indifference wasn't something Paula could live with. 'I'm sorry I couldn't visit earlier. So busy!' And then came the punch line: 'I had a breakdown. You didn't know, did you? Didn't make an effort to find out, did you? I lost a baby. Funny thing is I didn't want it in the first place. Babies have this knack of ruining one's body ... I don't think it had anything to do with the baby – the breakdown. It sounded good. It helped people understand why. I didn't know why. End of the line, burnout. I spent three months in a psychiatric unit. You have no idea what it does for one's career! Your shares go up. You're mad, deliciously mad. People love it! Are you comfortable, Mummy? Do they look after you?'

Mother's bottom lip was trembling, no more than usual, but Paula found it off-putting.

'Must dash! See you soon, promise ... now that Georgiana can't. Drink your tea.' She put her arms around Mother. It looked comical: Mother's osteoporosis-crunched torso, with her head protruding like a snail peering out of the shell, and Paula's artificial breasts in a push-up bra pushed into Mother's face, ready to asphyxiate her.

The breasts gave Mother a panic attack. She whimpered and tried to push Paula away. The image of female breasts was repugnant to her.

'You never really loved me, did you, Mummy?' Paula looked hurt. She was having to put up with her second rejection in one day. She blinked rapidly, warding off tears, and left. Her high heels drummed the floor like claps of thunder.

Mother didn't notice. She was looking at herself in a mirror. She was twelve, maybe thirteen. No longer the daring tomboy climbing trees and diving head-on into shallow brooks ... From her frown I could tell she didn't like what she saw, particularly her breasts. They were the sort of boobs Paula would kill for, or at the very least she would pay good money to have them installed upon her chest, but Mother hated them. Two foreign growths had invaded her body and restrained her freedom. She could not pass for a boy with hooters like that!

She was holding a roll of white elasticated bandage. She started under her left armpit and unfolded the roll across her chest, brutally squeezing her perky boobs. She went in circles, round and round her ribcage, and fastened the end with a safety pin.

Paula's flat was a shrine, mainly to herself. Her whole life (from the day she was born and carried home in a basket to a fairly recent photo of her under the arm of a man wearing a crown and stage make-up) was mapped out on the walls. There were framed pictures of Paula in her school plays, where she had appeared as anything from a sheep to Mary, the Mother of God. There was Paula in various stages of undress and body mass: receiving flowers, holding a knife to her chest over a stage lover's body; kissing somebody's cheek. There were a few autographed photographs of semi-famous actors: *To Paula xxx (signature illegible)*. They were all men. Not one single famous actress. There was one thing Paula had in common with Mother: the man fetish. If in a slightly different way.

Despite the exuberance with which Paula hung herself out for public view all over her flat, there was hardly anything else personal about her place. No pictures of life outside the theatre. No family photos. No weddings. No dogs. No holiday snapshots. No life. The only wedding photographs I saw, strewn on the floor, were mine!

Paula crossed the room, stabbing her high heels into those photographs. They were the ones I had sent to my nearest and dearest as a memento. My set was lovingly placed inside a white leather wedding album that nobody had opened in years. Paula's set was scattered on the floor, except for two: one was of Paula with Dad; the other one of Paula with Rob. Those two had made it to a table.

I was naturally outraged, but there was also something sinister about the way she had kept my wedding memories. There was something bordering on blasphemy. For the millionth time since my accident I wished I could do something. This time it was to sweep my photographs from the floor and take them home with me. Paula didn't deserve to have them.

She kicked off her high heels and shed layers of clothes as she walked to the bathroom. Her blood red lingerie had joined a heap of clothing on the floor. Her nakedness was frightening: skeletal and bruised. It had a wasted potential: a body of perfect female proportions which had been gutted and drained of blood, then pinned to the wall like one of Paula's impersonal pictures.

Paula did not share my opinion of her body. She ogled it lovingly in the mirror. The tips of her clawed fingers traversed lovingly from her neck and towards her artificially pumped-up boobs. Those were eerily rounded, like two tennis balls – clearly not the way Mother Nature intended them to be. Two incongruent attachments contrasting sadly with the rest of the matrix which was Paula's emaciated frame. As much as I found them travesties of nature, Paula found them endearing. She flicked and nudged them about playfully. 'Hello there, little soldiers!' she addressed them out loud, a glint of motherly pride in her eye. God! She must have been mad – talking to her own body parts! Her face dropped slightly when she focused her gaze on the nipples – they were crumpled and lifeless, little bits of Blu-Tac squashed out of shape. Expertly, Paula squeezed them between her fingers and twisted them back to life. They responded well to torture. Paula appeared pleased. She produced a wild shimmy which sent her tennis balls into a volley. 'Oh yes, come to Mama … grrr!'

She purred and adopted a sex kitten pose: one hand across her chest, allowing the tortured nipples to peer between her fingers; the other hand down into her loins, claws clutching her Brazilian tuft. She lifted her left knee and pointed her toes. 'Come on, you know you want me!'

she told herself. The woman was bonkers!

Her eyes abandoned her mean, lean midriff and reverted to her face. She pouted and kissed the air. Bared her teeth, ran her finger across the front row to remove a smudge of lipstick. She stuck her tongue out, and as there was little else to expose she exposed her tonsils and croaked out loud.

'Aaaah.'

She flicked her hair, extenuated her scruffy neck, and spoke in a theatrical manner, 'Hello there, lover! Take me as I am. Take me now … show me how much you want me …'

Brassy seduction suddenly discarded, her expression sobered up, her eyelashes flickered, and another Paula entered the stage: mild, wise, fragile Paula. She exhaled heavily, her voice softened. 'I've waited too,' she gasped. 'You weren't the only one. It felt like eternity, but we are together now.' She repeated her previous lines, but with a different twist. She pleaded softly, 'Don't be afraid. Take me. Take me as I am. Take me now … take me out of this hellhole! Save me!'

She caught her plaintive expression in the mirror, and laughed. Croaky, thunderous sound poured out of her throat. 'Don't be stupid! You couldn't save yourself …'

She began stuffing her lank hair into a plastic cap. A big lump of cotton wool dipped in makeup remover obliterated her face. Without accessories, for a split second the Paula I used to know made a brief appearance. She was still pretty in the sort of way that makes you think of the end of summer. She wouldn't know that: she wasn't looking in the mirror. Instead she twisted her body so that she could take a look at her skinny arse. She wiggled it frantically – a failed, pathetic attempt at middle-aged twerking. 'You know you want me,' she triumphed.

I was beginning to worry that soon she would descend into her own rendition of the *Vagina Monologues* so it was a relief when she immersed up to her neck in the foaming bath. I half expected to hear the clanking of her bones against the walls and floor of the bathtub, but she lay there, stiff and immobile, and with her eyes closed.

I waited, not sure where to go next. I didn't want to leave her on her own. She was a lonely, damaged creature. The 'in-between relationships' spiel was a lie. She had never had any relationships. It had for ever been Paula, and only Paula. Maybe I had failed her as a sister. I had always thought she was riding the wave of glamour and success and didn't need the burden of family to weigh her down. But I wasn't so sure any more. She was fragile. Very fragile. She was falling apart. As soon as I was out of hospital I would have to take her under my wing. To start with, a decent meal once a day would do wonders. I glanced at the photos of her from my wedding: fresh-faced little sister Paula. I could get her back to that point, it wasn't too late.

Then my eyes wandered to my own photos on the floor. And I discovered the savagery: in some of them Paula had drawn funny round glasses and moustaches on my face with a black marker; in others she had altogether obliterated my head. Mother got a pair of horns and a tail.

Dressed to kill, Paula emerged from her flat two hours later. She packed herself into Rob's Mini and drove to the Café Rouge. It was the same Café Rouge where I had met Tony on the day of my accident. Tony liked that place; it was within walking distance of his chambers. I liked that place too – it reminded me of Tony and his stag scent.

I shouldn't have been surprised to see Tony there. I shouldn't have been surprised to see Paula glide to his table and kiss him on the lips. But I was surprised, on both accounts. Those two together … it felt a bit incestuous.

OK, she'd said she knew him – God knows how and from where! – but knew him this well?? The kiss on the lips, her hand pawing at his neck ... I am talking serious physical intimacy. It was present in their body language. Paula wasn't putting on airs and graces, which she would be if she was chasing after a man. She knew this man. He was hers. Tony was equally relaxed: satiated. It was the sort of familiarity which would allow him to suggest a quickie in the loo in the safe knowledge that Paula would gladly oblige.

They had nothing to hide. All had been laid bare between them. A pang of jealously stung me and I had to remind myself it was me who had ended it with Tony.

'I saw Rob. Met the kids,' she told him.

'And?'

'The girl is obnoxious. The boy – bland. I didn't speak to him, couldn't be arsed.' Having my children referred to in such derogatory terms hurt. Coming from my sister it hurt even more. It added to the deposits of resentment and wariness of her I had been accumulating at the back of my mind since we were children.

'How are they taking it?'

'In one word?' She raised her right eyebrow. 'Chaos.'

'Did you see Georgie?'

'In passing. Doesn't look promising. The reality is: if she makes it, she'll be a vegetable.' I pretended not to hear it, not to take it to heart. Paula's medical expertise was thankfully non-existent. It was more wishful thinking than a diagnosis. But every word she uttered hurt.

'I ...' Tony sighed heavily.

'Don't tell me you miss her?'

'Never mind. I have you,' he grinned with a cheeky boy's wink.

Gratified, Paula purred and put her hand on his knee. 'You can have me if you ask nicely.'

'You know I'm not in the habit of asking.'

It was at this point that I expected her to break into, 'Then take me. Take me as I am.' Oddly, she didn't do that. Obviously her earlier rehearsal was not meant for Tony. Instead she said, 'The police came by when I was there.'

'Oh?'

'They think it wasn't an accident. They surmised that it was planned. They have the boy's picture. Unclear, though.'

'A boy? You can tell it was a boy?'

'You can tell much more than that, I guess. If you know who to look for. Are you looking for a boy? Or for a girl?' Ha! Here she was – back on form! You can't teach an old dog new tricks. Paula was Paula. To my immense satisfaction it turned out Tony was looking for neither. He told her he had to go: just like that – out of the blue.

By the time he got to the club, Tony was drunk. I had watched him drink alone at home. He would raise a glass to his reflection in the mirror and each time salute himself with a cheery *'Fuck you'*. He wasn't a graceful drinker. He was drinking vodka, neat. The bottle stood on the table next to an ashtray and a packet of cigarettes. I never knew Tony to be a smoker, but he was a seasoned one. The way he held a cigarette reminded me of juvenile delinquents – he held it between his forefinger and thumb, cupped in his hand, and he sucked on it in gulps as if he was afraid of being caught.

Despite our sordid affair I had never been to Tony's house. We had both kept our respective family nests off bounds so they wouldn't be soiled. Except that his wasn't a family nest. It was something altogether different. It was large and pretentious. It had wood-panelled walls and an impressive library filled with leather-bound tomes and first editions. In his bedroom he had a four-poster bed with a carved headboard. In the hallway there was a display cabinet full of pistols and weapons tucked away lovingly upon dark green damask. The sitting room boasted an oil portrait of a rather attractive woman in a ball gown with a sixties hairdo, and another one of Tony. The entire house gave the distinct impression of being a gentleman's residence. It was so overcooked that I was convinced Tony was taking the piss out of himself. And by the time I finished nosing about his home, he was pretty pissed too. He pulled off his tie and undid the top button of his immaculately white shirt. Thus dishevelled (by Tony's standards), he went to the garage and jumped into a magnificent MGA convertible. His white shirt went beautifully with its black leather seats.

Considering the amount of alcohol in his bloodstream, he drove better than most of us do sober. He parked two streets away from the club and covered the distance on foot. And there we were: in a seedy basement club oozing sex, depravity, and money. In other words: an urban gentlemen's club.

Tony found a place by the bar and ordered a drink. For a while he watched a pole dancer, a well-endowed siren with an incredibly flexible spine. The music in the background was jazzy; the red lighting unashamedly brothel-esque.

A woman wearing a low-backed sequin dress planted herself next to Tony and asked him for a drink. I gathered she had to be at least £300 an hour and marvelled why on earth Tony would choose to pay for sex if he could have it free of charge with any woman he set his eyes on. The added value factor of potential venereal diseases must have played a part.

He ordered her a drink and – with a pleasant smile – told her to piss off. I felt reassured. Perhaps he was there for the music.

When he downed his own drink, he edged towards a young man sitting in an obscure corner of the bar with his legs crossed. He was so young milk was dripping from his nose. He was wearing a tight T-shirt with a print that said:

I don't come cheap. Surely, I thought, Tony was going to ask the male prostitute where the toilets were. Tony liked women, I knew that for a fact.

'Do you do home visits?' Tony asked. The toilet was obviously the last thing on his mind.

'For a price, and a taxi fare back here,' the boy stretched. On close inspection I could tell he was wearing thick foundation and wasn't yet shaving regularly. His eyelashes were elongated with black mascara. They reminded me of Emma, but I quickly banished that parallel from my mind. He batted his eyelashes. His pupils were huge.

'Follow me. Keep a distance.'

Somehow I felt less resentful about seeing Tony with another man than I had when I first saw him with my own sister. That is not to say that I wasn't shocked. All that crap about the laws of nature, abominations, and travesties crossed my mind as I watched those two, stark naked, indulging in an act of same-sex intercourse. To be accurate, Tony was indulging; the young man looked more like he was enduring. The roles of the dominant and the submissive were clearly delineated. To put it bluntly, Tony was doing all the fucking and the young man was putting up with it. Obviously for money and little else. Pleasure didn't come into it for the poor bugger. I wondered if Tony had realised that or whether in his macho, egomaniac mind he believed he was doing the boy a sexual favour. It was hard to tell. Right through the act, just like in those days when he did it with me, his face showed no emotion. It was as if his mind was blanking out his actions. Tony was a sexual sphinx.

When he finished, he rolled off the boy's backside and scrambled under the bed. The young man gazed after him with mild curiosity. He was also pulling on his trousers, struggling with his fly, tugging at it with shaky fingers.

You could taste his discomfort: he was ashamed and wanted to cover his nakedness and forget all about it. Clearly, the young man wasn't gay out of choice. There was probably a girlfriend somewhere in the back of his cupboard, a pretty thing kept in the dark about her man's sources of income.

'About the money,' he said quietly, his earlier cockiness gone with the wind.

'In a napkin holder on the table. In the kitchen.'

Tony returned with a whip. It was a just an ordinary horse riding whip, nothing kinky, and perhaps that's why it sent a shiver down my spine. The young boy winced. 'You didn't say anything about –'

'That'd spoil the fun, now, wouldn't it?'

'I don't do that stuff. Keep the money,' the boy was visibly scared. He was trying hurriedly to get his T-shirt on.

Tony towered over him in his masculinity and his unabashed nakedness. He passed the whip to the boy. 'Hit me with it.'

The boy picked it up. He looked surprised. 'What? Now?' I, too, thought the whipping stuff came before, not after, the fornication. Some sort of deviant, back-to-front foreplay if old wives' tales were anything to go by.

'Now. You want to hit me, don't you?'

The young man must have seen it all in his line of work, yet he was uncertain. There was something unconventional about the sequence of events here. He stared at Tony, calculating if hitting him, as he had asked, would lead to retaliation, and then, how far the escalation of violence would go. The boy's pupils were still dilated, making his eyes look as if there were huge holes in them.

'Hit me, you twat! You know you want to. I fucked you and you didn't want to be fucked. Even for the money … If your girl knew, she'd be sick. Hit me. Don't be a wimp.'

Tony raised his hand and, defensively, the young man

raised the whip. He struck. It got Tony on the forearm. He smiled.

'Is that all you've got? I didn't feel a thing.'

The boy struck again. And again. With each strike, he became more forceful. All his strength and all his anger went into punishing Tony. In the end, they both collapsed on the bed, spent.

A couple of hours later the young man got up. He listened to Tony's breathing with his ear to his mouth. He examined the bruises on his back. There were a couple of deeper cuts, but mainly there were just angry red stripes. Strangely, there was no sign of any earlier scars. It had to be the first time for Tony. Quietly, the young man collected his socks and shoes and tiptoed barefoot out of the bedroom. He found the money folded neatly inside a napkin holder on the kitchen table. He counted the cash and put it in his trouser pocket. That was when he saw the watch. It was a gold Cartier with a brown leather strap, worth a good few thousand pounds. He put it on his wrist; admired it briefly against the light; took it off and placed it back on the table. He squatted to put on his socks and trainers. Before leaving, he stole another glance at the watch. It took him a few seconds to think about it. Chances were he would bump into Tony again, at the club. Still, the temptation was greater: he swiped the watch and put it into his pocket.

'I'm a light sleeper,' Tony was at the bottom of the stairs in the hallway. He was wearing a dressing gown.

'Sorry I woke you up. I found the money, thanks.'

'Do you want to call a taxi?'

'No, I'll walk. Keep the money and walk.'

'Very prudent of you … before you go, I was wondering if you'd like to see my pistol collection.'

'Not into guns, sorry.'

'Nevertheless, I'll show you.' Tony put his arm around

the boy. On the face of it, it was a friendly gesture, but in reality it wasn't friendly at all. It was an order. The boy was marched to the display cabinet. Tony took a key out of a small wooden box and opened the cabinet. He picked up a pair of identical pistols and passed them both to the boy who held them awkwardly as if they were about to go off. 'My favourite: a pair of 20-bore Bohemian flint pistols. Mid-eighteenth century. Just look at the side-plates. Can you see? Amazing scene – cavalrymen in combat. If they could tell a story, what story would they tell?' Tony marvelled. 'Look at the craftsmanship. They don't make things like that any more. Be careful!' he relieved the boy of the weapons and placed them back in the display case. 'I paid over ten thousand pounds for them. An excellent investment. And this one here,' he passed another gun to the poor bugger, 'is a Parabellum POW Krieghoff, German, 1937. I love this one here, Makarov, Russian … what's special about it is that it is the silenced version. You wouldn't hear the shot, just a "puff". Want to hold it? It isn't loaded.'

The boy took it.

'Now to this one,' Tony was holding a pretty ordinary and modern-looking gun. He cocked it. 'I won't let you have this one because this one is loaded. I got it from a client of mine. Nasty piece of work, but he was grateful and wanted to show his gratitude … Never know when it may come in handy,' he said. It isn't licensed. Officially it doesn't exist. If I used it, it couldn't be traced back to me or anyone else.' He was pointing the gun at the boy's stomach. 'If I shot you with this gun and dumped your body somewhere quiet, no one would be any wiser … so why don't we start again? So we can be friends … we'll go back to the kitchen and you'll put on the table something that you found there that doesn't belong to you. Does that sound like a deal?'

The young man nodded slowly. He reached into his

pocket and took out the watch. He passed it to Tony.

'No. On the table. That's where you found it, correct?'

They went to the kitchen. The boy did as he was told. Tony picked up the watch, looked at it and placed it back on the table. Sliding his unlicensed gun into his dressing-gown pocket, he sat down and bid the youth to do the same. The young man complied.

'That's better,' Tony smiled. He offered the boy a cigarette from his packet on the table, but the boy declined.

'I don't smoke, sorry.'

'Mind if I do?'

The boy shook his head. Tony lit a cigarette. 'Would you believe me if I told you I was just like you? My mother died when I was eighteen. Cancer. Single parent. She was an artist, free spirit. No husband. No means, you know the kind? Adorable, really!' Tony took a sip of vodka from the bottle and passed the bottle to the young man. 'Drink.' The youth did. Tony watched him put the bottle down on the table. 'I was just about to start my first year, reading Law. Whoring myself was the easiest way of getting by. I had the grooming, just didn't have the money to go with it.'

Tony! A rent boy! Well, it shouldn't surprise me that much. After all, in our profession we always sell ourselves to the highest bidder. For Tony it must've been a natural progression.

'So you see, my man, I was just like you …' He drilled the boy with a steely gaze. 'I imagine you have a life outside the club?'

'I'm doing Psychology.'

'Psychology? Wow! Girlfriend?'

'Yes.'

'I knew you weren't queer. None of us is. Just a means to an end.' Tony stubbed his cigarette. 'Except that, unlike you, I didn't go around thieving from my clients. I was grateful to them. They put me through a Law degree. And they were grateful to me too: for being discreet. We're good friends now. They helped me. I helped them. We still help each other. It's a small world out there ... did you really think I wouldn't find you?'

'Sorry. I don't know what I was thinking.'

'You have to learn quickly in this profession or sooner or later your arse will wash up on a beach somewhere around Weston-super-Mare. Do you understand?'

'I think I do.'

'You have a name?'

'Etienne.'

'Etienne, huh? Stage name, then. Your real name must be something like Jack or Sam. Etienne will do for me. Etienne is a nice courtesan's name: pliable, gentle ...'

'I want to get out of this business. I don't want to do this.'

'The sooner you learn to do it well, the sooner you can get out of doing it,' Tony smiled. He slid his Cartier across the table, to the boy. 'Take it. And next time, just ask nicely. Don't accept less than three grand for it.'

The boy looked, incredulous.

'Take it, I said. It's a gift – we're friends. Take it and get out.'

Rob and Mark took it in turns to sit by my bedside. I was glad of their company. It was a refreshing change after Tony, as if I had crossed from Purgatory back into the land of the living. You would think that hospital wasn't quite the place to live life to the fullest considering that most of its residents were half-dead already, but Tony was dead through and through. He was the Devil incarnate, if you believed in such things. The thought that there had been a time when I consorted with him filled me with dread. I had never really known the man; I hadn't known I was playing with fire. I was relieved it was over. Rob and Mark, sitting by my bedside, were my guarantee of sanity. I still had a family: a loving husband and two amazing kids. Nothing was lost. I just had to get my arse into gear, and get better. I had so much to live for.

'How is she?' Mark asked.

'No change.'

'Did you speak to the doctor?'

'He hasn't got much to say. They'll do a MRI scan on Monday. They'll know something then.'

'You look like shit. Go home, Dad. Get some sleep. I'll sit here for a bit.'

'I think I'll go back to work tomorrow. This waiting is doing my head in.'

I stayed with Mark. I couldn't help noticing that he had put on a fresh T-shirt which said: *Drab and proud of it.* He also smelled of cologne and was clean-shaven. Gel-set, his fringe was stiffened into flamboyant rigor mortis. I realised he was hoping for a fix of Chi. The nurse that walked in was anything but Chi. She was middle-aged and plain, not too tall, not too short, not too skinny and not too fat – the sort of non-entity you could only describe in negatives. Mark glanced at her, hopefully at first, then instantly deflated. She went on with my chart updates; Mark took out his mobile. It came to life with a ding-dong. Unlike Chi, this nurse didn't tell him to switch it off. He checked for messages. There weren't any. He typed one to Charlotte: *Soz 4 being an rs. C u swn? X*

The nurse had left. Mark watched her close the door behind her. He made sure his message had gone. He stared at his silent mobile and kept on waking it each time it went to sleep. 'What was I thinking?' he asked me. I wished I knew and could tell him. I was ecstatic he talked to me. Someone did at last. Recently, people tended to talk about me rather than to me.

At last the telephone whooshed in a message. It was from Charlotte: *Cum now silly X*

I wasn't sure which kind of *cum* she had in mind, but Mark was in the know. He keyed in: *On my way X*

To me he said, 'See you, Mum!'

Charlotte's mother opened the door. She was all smiles, smelled of talcum powder, and wore fresh lipstick: it shone like a dung beetle's backside.

'Mark! Come in! Char's upstairs.'

Mark was taken aback. It was close to midnight, yet the house was lit from head to toe and Mrs Palmer looked fresh as a daisy. 'I hope it's not too late. Maybe I should come back tomorrow.'

'Don't be silly! Come in. We're practically family!'

She led him to the sitting room where Mr Palmer sat stiffly, pretending to be reading a newspaper. I knew he was only pretending because his reading glasses were on top of his head.

'Steve, look who's here!'

Feigning surprise, Mr Palmer got to his feet, shook Mark's hand and patted him on the back, mumbling his delight. There was a white toothpaste ring around his lips. 'We were just about to …'

He gazed helplessly at his wife. She smiled a full-toothed smile. 'Tea?'

'Beer?' countered Mr Palmer. 'I was about to get one for myself?'

'Beer'd be good, thanks. Is Charlotte –'

'Oh, she's coming,' Mrs Palmer was beaming. Mr Palmer shuffled to the kitchen for the beers.

'Maybe I should go upstairs?' Mark offered.

'Oh no! She'll be here in a minute.' Mrs Palmer winked and continued to brandish her teeth. 'She wants to tell us something. Whatever that may be …'

'Sorry it's a bit warm,' Mr Palmer handed a bottle to Mark that had never seen the inside of a fridge. I knew how much Mark hated warm beer. *I'd rather drink my own piss*, I had heard him say once, and though I didn't like the language I shared the sentiment.

Charlotte saved the day. She rolled downstairs, smelling of roses. She was wearing a dress, which looked a bit too short for her: not the mini-type short, but the grown-out-of short. The waistline was right under her armpits. Trying to be feminine, she looked way out of her depth. She sat next to Mark, cornering him on the sofa. She kissed him.

'You've been a bad boy, silly!'

'Sorry … been out of sorts.'

'So what is it you wanted to tell us?' her mother provided a cue.

Charlotte extended her left hand. A sizeable diamond glistened on her fourth finger.

'Is it what I think it is?' Mrs Palmer was breathless.

'We're engaged!' There was a childlike delight in Charlotte's eyes. She couldn't control her face: it was sparkling, like her diamond. Her mother had tears of joy in her eyes. Mr Palmer was mumbling something to the effect of 'I never!' and 'Well done!' I felt moved to tears myself and wished I were there in body, not just in spirit. At first baffled, Mark had quickly turned a corner, and smiled. I thought he was happy. He looked happy now that the announcement was done with and, after all, the sky didn't fall on his head.

'We're engaged, yes. There you go.'

'Champagne is in order!' shouted Mrs Palmer, and in no time a bottle of Brut on ice, in a misty silver bucket, materialised on the table. The clinking of glasses and jibber-jabber of congratulations and exclamations went on for a few exulted minutes, and then the newly engaged couple headed for the upstairs bedroom. Obviously, a good romp was on the cards, but I thought I would leave them to it. I had had enough sex for one day, and I craved nothing more than to lie quietly next to my snoring spouse.

Not surprisingly Mark appeared a little dishevelled when he turned up at the hospital in the morning. It was a welcome sight: the boy had come to his senses. A bit of hanky-panky for a young, red-blooded man was what the doctors had ordered. I could see a marked improvement in his complexion alone. Charlotte was good for him. A tenacious wife is the next best thing after a tenacious mother. Mark had both – or at least he would soon – and he would go far in life. He wouldn't have to whore himself like Tony had; he wouldn't end up damaged like Tony had. Despite that little wobble earlier on, Mark would continue on a straight and narrow trajectory to a respectable life. The trials and tribulations would, fingers crossed, miss him altogether.

He was just about to come and tell me all about it, when Chi passed him in the corridor. Without her nurse's uniform she looked even more like a pre-pubescent girl than before. She was wearing a sleeveless tunic and a pair of striped leggings. Her hair hung loose to her waist. It had an unnatural shine to it. She didn't see Mark, but he did see her and decided to follow her.

Why? I silently asked him.

Her steps were small and her feet pointed slightly inwards. She was deep in thought. Like a seasoned MI5 agent, Mark let her go as far as the next street corner, then ran after her. He watched her stop at a pedestrian crossing and wait for the green light. As soon as she was on the other side, he launched himself across the busy street, forcing a Royal Mail van to come to a screeching halt and a few other drivers to punch their horns and deliver a unanimous verdict of 'Wanker!'

No! I screamed. Another hit-and-run in the family in the same week was bound to finish me off.

Mark got on the same bus as the Vietnamese nurse. He sat four seats behind her, his eyes fixed on the back of her head. *What was he thinking?*

They alighted in Staple Hill. The street they dived into was a deserted, tired-looking row of uninspiring terrace houses perched directly on the pavement, with no front gardens to speak of and all cars parked tightly in the street, leaving space for only one-way traffic. Chi stopped, stooped, and fumbled in her bag, presumably looking for her house key. Only now did I notice her bag: it was intensely oriental in style with an image of an elephant embroidered in brightly coloured wool onto green canvas. She was also wearing slip-ons with big orange flowers perched on the straps. All of a sudden I wasn't looking at that common species, humble foreign nurse, but at an exotic creature, bursting with colour and mystique.

'Why are you stalking me?' She was glaring at Mark, a small can in her hand, pointing at his face.

'I am … um … um …' Mark explained, rather eloquently.

'You have been following me.'

'Well … I-ah … Well, yes.'

'Why you've been following me?'

'Remember me? From the hospital? You're looking after my mum. Only last night you didn't turn up.' Mark was beginning to gather his wits. He made a few steps forward.

'Don't. This is pepper spray.' She waved the can in his face.

'Yes …' he backed off. 'I just wanted to see where you lived. That's all.'

'Why?'

'Well … Simply … I don't know why,' he gave up.

'Go away.'

He didn't move.

'I was waiting for you last night. You didn't come. I thought I made you up. And then I saw you, couldn't believe my eyes –'

'All European men say that, I've been warned. Go

away or I will call the police.'

'I did a stupid thing because of that.' He didn't seem to hear the threat. The last thing I wanted was for my son to be arrested for stalking a nurse. I was urging him to turn on his heel and go.

'Because of what?'

'Because I thought I … made you up. Well, not really, but since you didn't turn up I thought, "What are you doing, man! Get a life!" And then I did a stupid thing.'

'That's my fault? The stupid thing that you did?'

'Not entirely. I'm to blame, too,' he admitted.

She laughed.

He laughed. 'I probably sound like a total jerk.'

'You do.'

'Look, can I just speak to you? I just need to speak to you. I promise I won't –'

'Why speak to me?'

'I really don't know. But I have to.'

'Is it about your mother? Because –'

'No. It's about you. I want to speak about you. I want to know about you. Bloody hell! What I'm really doing here is asking you on a date! How about that?'

'Am I supposed to be impressed?'

'No! Just … say yes?'

'I'm tired. I'm going to bed and you're not invited.'

'I never said … Please don't run away!'

'I just said: I'm going to bed. I've been working all night. I'm tired.'

'Well, I'll sit here and wait.' Mark slumped onto the pavement and sat with his feet wide apart. From the depths of his pocket his mobile whooshed in a text message. The nurse tilted her head.

'Are you not going to answer that?'

'No.' he took out his phone, pressed a button, and blew over the thing as if it was the barrel of a smoking gun. The text message so extinguished, he put the phone back in his pocket. 'I'll be here, when you're ready.'

She shrugged and walked to the front door. It took her a while to find the key. She turned it slowly in the lock. One last glance over her shoulder. Mark was still there, like a piece of litter on the pavement. She took pity on him, which I wished to God she hadn't. She said, 'I will be up at six.'

The instant I saw them together I knew they were very close. It was in their body language, in their eyes when they looked at each other and in the way they spoke to each other: short sentences where more was left out than was said. This woman had to be very important to Rob, but I had never heard of her. Had I not been listening, or had he not been telling me? Granted, Rob hardly spoke of his work; it was a distant place, a necessary evil; it was a place without a soul. Drafting policy and bylaws isn't exactly the most exciting topic for conversation. I never asked either. I didn't have the time to listen to answers. And I wasn't interested. I couldn't imagine what there would be, in Rob's job, to inspire my curiosity. Plus, I trusted him. Rob wasn't the type to harbour secrets. He wasn't the type to live a double life. He had enough trouble living a single one! For God's sake, he was a man clinging to a domestic kettle for comfort!

He had his garden to tend to, muddy overalls, threadbare socks, green fingers, rows of carrots and baskets of sweet williams. He was afraid of life! He dreaded school runs, had lost countless umbrellas on the bus, and for the past twenty years had taken Rob-only annual holidays at the same bed & breakfast in Cornwall. Even the Cornish cows must have been bored stiff watching him crossing the same plains, using the same path, day in and day out – invariably in the second week of September when all the awkward kids were back at school. Rob did not do sordid affairs. He didn't have it in him.

Perhaps I was overreacting. Perhaps I had never heard of that woman because there was nothing to tell. She was just a work colleague with a sympathetic ear, forgotten every day the moment my husband stepped out of the office and caught a bus home to me.

She was, after all, a remarkably unremarkable person. Short and chubby, she had full hips overflowing like melting butter into her gelatinous thighs. Her arms were wobbly and her fingers – little chorizos. There was no wedding ring on the fourth chorizo of her left hand. Her blonde hair was tied in a bun with a few stray wisps curling around her ears. It was her face that I found unnerving. It radiated warmth. Perhaps it was in her full-lipped smile; perhaps in her innocently baby-blue eyes. Perhaps it was in the chubby cheeks, fresh and shiny like said baby's bottom. The more I looked at her, the calmer I became. This wasn't your typical vamp man-eater. Sex with her would be like scones with butter and strawberry jam. Conventional and predictable. She was a mother figure: Mother Earth in full-brief knickers and socks in bed.

So that was Rob's jealously guarded secret. I relaxed. My first impression was patently wrong. Could it be, I pondered, my very own guilty conscience playing tricks on me?

They were sitting in a vast, open-plan office with twenty other office moles, each one looking just like the next: men in boring grey suits, women with sensible haircuts and comfortable footwear. They were so alike that they could become invisible and nothing would have changed. Even though they all shared this space, they didn't seem to be distracted in any way by the presence of the others, by their voices or actions. Maybe they weren't moles; maybe they were busy bees, the immaculate worker type that lives to work and works to live.

Rob had brought a file of papers in a brown manila

folder. It was lying between him and the woman like an acceptable excuse for a breach of protocol. He was sitting on a swivel chair, angled towards the woman. She wasn't facing her desk; she was facing him.

'You don't think you came back too early, Robert?' she asked, and quickly put her chorizo bunch on his shoulder and peered into his eyes with an apologetic smile that could pass for angelic. 'Not that I'm not glad to see you back, but ... are you ready? This is a madhouse.'

'I can't do anything standing over her bed. It's debilitating. I'm powerless waiting ...'

'I'm sorry, I can't possibly imagine how bad it is.'

'I'd rather be at work, talk to people, act normal. Time goes faster.'

'If that helps ... If there's anything I can do? I hope you know?'

'I need a good friend, Olivia. To talk to ... '

'I'll listen, if that's all I can do. Any time, you know that.'

'There are things I didn't tell the kids, didn't tell anyone. I'm pretending that I myself don't know how hopeless it is.'

'Pretending is like having faith,' the angel in her was coming out of the closet as we spoke – as *they* spoke. I could almost understand why Rob needed her. 'Power of mind, they say, performs miracles. If you have faith, if you keep pretending, it may never come to the worst.'

'What would be the worst thing to happen, Olivia? I've been wondering about that. Is it her dying? Or is there something worse?'

'You want her to pull through, that's the first thing,' the woman called Olivia told my husband firmly, as if it was something he didn't understand and therefore had to learn by heart, like the Ten Commandments.

'Had a word with the doctor. Georgie may well live if she's got this far. Three days is a long time in terms of medical emergency.'

'That's a good thing. It's a start.'

'But the brain damage, you see?' He reached for her hand. No one else saw it but me. 'Everything adds up: the swelling, the cells that have already died and those that are still dying ... parts of the brain – vanquished ... there's a fifty-fifty chance she'll be brain –'

Rob swallowed the last word, but we all knew the word was *dead*. Brain dead. I made an educated guess: that equated to the IQ of an amoeba.

I felt the need to sit with someone who had absolutely nothing to say, and nothing to surprise me with. I went to see Mother. She was still – or already – up, and in her favourite chair, wearing milky-beige stockings twisted at her ankles, and mumbling under her breath without making a sound. The stale biscuit was there too – her faithful companion. Three days ago I would have complained – would've raised hell. Three days ago I would have sued the management for negligence; today I thought of the stale biscuit as part of the background in a slow-moving setting of growing out of life gracefully. A reassuring biscuit that puts everything into perspective. I smiled at the thing.

In that world of her own, Mother was somewhere in her early thirties and she was contriving her first night with Dad. Late bloomer in those days, but I guess first and foremost Mother was a career woman, like me. She must've given in to the pressures of social convention later in life. Maybe her biological clock started ticking.

It was a date, not a first one; they had been seeing each other for a few months. Nothing strenuous: just holding hands and sharing candy-floss at a funfair; no exchange of bodily fluids had taken place yet other than saliva on the lemonade bottle they took swigs from in turns.

I knew Mother had entered the dating scene late in life

by the swinging sixties' standards. I knew her original plan had been to join the police force. I knew she had even made progress towards the rank of detective constable, but then something had gone awry and out of the blue she'd abandoned the career path which was an unorthodox one for a woman in those days, but very much Mother. She had abandoned it in favour of becoming a well-grounded housewife. I remember speculating as to what had made her forsake her dreams, and I concluded she had fallen in love. With Dad. It was such a romantic notion and it had always, invariably, reaffirmed my faith in the sanctity of marriage.

Mother was going to do it: she was going to have sex with Dad – *give herself to him*, as they would put it aptly in those days. She had bought a new pair of silk stockings and a new bra with matching suspender belt for the occasion, and sprinkled herself with Yardley's English Rose body fragrance from groin to armpit. Her lips were lusciously red; her dress (so unlike her!) was well … a DRESS! Nothing would have been particularly odd about this ritual and about her decision – millions of women had gone for premarital sex before her and even more would do it after her. What was odd however was her timing. Her period had just started. She examined the blood on the old pad and threw it into a fire blazing in the coal stove. She wanted blood to be there when she gave herself to Dad. She wanted him to think she was a virgin, which made me realise that she wasn't. I was astonished. She had been forever telling me and Paula about '*saving ourselves for the right man*'. She would forever put herself forward as our role model: the virgin Joan of Arc! Paula had failed spectacularly to heed Mother's recommendations, but I had taken them well to heart. I was now heavily underwhelmed as I watched her scheme and simulate her own virginity. I felt cheated, on Dad's behalf. She had *given herself* to someone else before him and made him think he was the only one ... What an anti-climax! Was nothing sacred anymore? I must say I had lost a good chunk of the reverence I had for Mother and I even began to think that it was Paula, not me, who had taken after her. Maybe, I was Dad's girl after all?

There was a knock on the door and Mother went to open it. Dad stood there: young, dashing, smiling, hopeful. 'You look smashing,' he said.

I decided to go home. Watching my parents have sex wasn't at the top of my list of things to do before I die.

The cat was sitting on the fence. He adopted his usual imperious pose as he scanned the neighbourhood for signs of intrusion. An old, battered Kia stopped outside the house. The cat whipped its tail with mild irritation. He looked displeased. Anyone with an ounce of taste would be displeased. The Kia was a repulsive green. Blistering rust was creeping up the fenders. The thing had to be at least twenty years old, unsafe to push around the sandpit, never mind be unleashed on public roads! Yet it had been driven to our house by Brandon the Paleontological Chef. On board was my daughter. She had her school bag on her lap, which gave me hope she had been to school in the morning.

'I don't want to go home, Brandon, please!'

'I've got to go to work. Someone has to work, yeah?'

'The so-called auntie must still be there. I don't want to see her.' Emma punched a little green Christmas tree air refresher hanging from the rear view mirror. The tree orbited the mirror, then rested.

'We can go and check.' On closer inspection, the boy was a wimp. Emma chose her men wisely.

'And then what? You'll leave me there. I want to go with you. I promise I'll be no trouble.'

Brandon lit a cigarette. He blew the smoke out the window. 'Your dad will be worried where you are.'

'Right now Dad doesn't know what day of the week it is. He won't notice me gone.'

'No, we can't do that to him.'

Both Emma and I could see he was yielding under pressure. She resolutely refused to get out of the car, and waited. Brandon finished his cigarette and flicked the butt out of the window. 'OK then, but there are some conditions ...'

'Anything!'

'You'll have to bring your books with you and do some revision, yeah?'

'Yep.'

'And you'll introduce me to your dad. So that he knows where you are. As in: in safe hands.'

Emma exhaled like a pricked balloon. 'You're sure you're up to meeting my parents?'

'Em, I want to do it right. I feel shit, hiding in shadows, like we're criminals. We don't want them to find out the wrong way, do we?'

'I don't care if they don't find out at all!'

'But I do. Anyway, it's just your dad. You said he was harmless. Let's face it, Em, it's your mum who was the issue. You said she'd have had a problem with me. You said she'd have a cardiac arrest if she knew about us. Well, she's already had a cardiac. She's sort of out of the way, no offence intended!' *None taken, humph*! 'So it's down to your dad. Is he going to mind me?'

'Dad doesn't mind anything and if he does, he'll be too polite to say.'

'So, let's do it. We'll all feel better for it.'

I don't think Rob registered anything that happened in the next two minutes. It had not taken more than two minutes for Emma to burst in with Brandon in tow. Rob was in the kitchen, trying – in vain – to make cheese on toast. He had put both the bread and the cheese directly into the toaster.

The cheese started melting and burning inside it. The smoke activated the alarm. It was wailing while Rob was waving a tea towel in front of the detector.

'The windows!' Brandon sprang into action, opening the kitchen window and pushing open the front door to let the smoke out. Without a word to her dad, Emma shot straight up the stairs to her room to fetch her books. The alarm stopped. Rob and Brandon found themselves face to face in the narrow landing under the smoke detector.

'Thank you! I never … I mean … I thought I'd have cheese on toast. What could be simpler? Well … It got a bit out of hand. Sorry about that,' Rob was stammering. 'I'm sure you've got more important … I mean real emergencies. You are a fireman?'

'No Dad!' Emma was back with a couple of thick volumes under her arm. 'He's my boyfriend. Brandon – Dad; Dad – Brandon.'

Rob looked like he needed his kettle. 'Oh, I see. Not a fireman? Yes, of course. How could a fireman arrive so quickly? A boyfriend, Brandon … Naturally! Pleased to meet you at last. Emma's told me so much about you I feel I know you.' He was shaking the young man's hand with great vigour. It was civility taken way too far in my humble opinion, but then no one seemed to concern themselves with my opinions any more.

'Brandon isn't a fireman. Where did you get that idea from? He is a palaeontologist.'

'Dubbing as a chef,' Brandon chirped in and returned Rob's enthusiastic handshake.

'I'm afraid I can't offer you anything to –'

'I have to be going. My shift's about to start. Just quickly: I work in *La Rochelle*.'

'*La Rochelle*? Is that …'

'It's a restaurant in Broadmead. I thought you ought to know something about me. Kind of.'

'So you're the fireman?'

'He's a chef, Dad!'

'I thought you said a fireman.'

'No, you keep on about a fireman! Brandon is a palaeontologist!'

'Not a chef, then?'

'I am a chef, sir.' Clearly Brandon felt compelled to intervene before the debate got out of hand. 'I'll take Emma with me, if that's OK with you. She'll get something decent to eat at the restaurant.' Brandon gazed at the blackened toaster. 'I'll bring her back home after ten.'

Emma was already out of the door. 'See you, Dad!'

Brandon pointed at the toaster. 'It'll trip your mains if you try to use it again. Why don't you try the grill instead?'

'The grill.' Rob looked inspired.

'It was nice to meet you,' Brandon assured Rob, and promptly retreated after Emma.

'Sorry about the trouble. I'll definitely try the grill.'

Mark brushed by Rob at the front door. He too was on his way out. Freshly out of the bath, he left behind a trail of Radox Original body wash. His hair was still wet. His *Drab and Proud of It* T-shirt was replaced with its faithful grey replica stating *I'm a terrorist.*

'Can I borrow your car, Dad?' Mark opened the garage. It was empty. 'Where *is* your car?' Only I and Paula knew where the Mini had gone. Rob looked both puzzled and apologetic for his ignorance. He went to the garage to look for himself. He checked around carefully as if, by any chance, the car could have crawled under the box with screws and nails.

'My car?'

'Yes! The Mini. I am in a hurry, Dad.'

'I don't know. I think I may have left it at work. No, hang on – I took a bus to work. No, no … Is it stolen, do

103

you think?'

'I've no time to think. I'm late.'

'Perhaps I should report it stolen?'

'Perhaps you should. I'll take Mum's car. Is it OK if I do? You're not going anywhere, are you?'

My car was parked in front of the second door of our double garage. They all knew I didn't like anyone to drive it but me. Rob's car, when it was being used, was normally on loan to either friends or family, or any odd stray cat in the neighbourhood. I cringed at my car being used without my permission: the seat being moved, the mirrors repositioned, an intruder helping himself to my Softmints. Rob hesitated.

'I don't think Mum would like that.'

'It's not like she's going to need it tonight.'

'I suppose what she doesn't know won't hurt her.'

'Thanks, Dad. Oh, and can I get a small loan? Fifty quid?'

Rob patted himself on his chest and buttocks, in all those places where a wallet should be. 'Um ... I seem to have misplaced my wallet.'

'Stolen? Like the car? Never mind, I'll starve.'

They were sitting on a bench by the quayside, eating fish and chips. I'd half expected Chi to tackle chips with chopsticks, or at least a knife and fork, but she was quite efficient eating with her fingers. Behind them was a fancy restaurant with glass walls and yellow lanterns whose light reflected in the water, rippled and smudged on the oily black surface. There was a gentle but nippy breeze coming from the river. Neither of them seemed to mind or even notice it. Mark looked exhilarated. You would think it was he who had died and gone to heaven. He joked. He laughed – genuinely laughed. He fooled around. I never knew him to be this carefree. Mark had always been a very serious young man, or perhaps – it occurred to me as I

104

watched him now – he hadn't been a happy one. He had a steady girl whom he had dated for four years. There was sex in it and a meeting of minds, surely. And yet it seemed that until now he simply went with the flow because he didn't know any differently. Until one day, dutiful and anxious, he had gone to visit his dying mother in hospital, and incidentally bumped into his very own Yoko Ono. And all of a sudden he was John Lennon: avant-garde and shamelessly intoxicated. The extent of his happiness could be measured by the amount of ketchup he put on his chips: copious. The chips were bathed in sauce.

'Does Chi stand for anything?'

'Does Mark?'

'Some saint or other.'

'Chi is nothing as noble. It stands for a branch, a twig.'

'Twiggy, in English?'

'It may break.' Her eyes belied her words. There was steely determination in them. Perhaps it was the shape or the heavy hoods of eyelids that made her appear stronger than him despite everything: her size, her displacement and her childlike pronunciation. I was looking at her and I remembered an image I once saw. A little Vietnamese girl, running away from pain, naked, a mist of napalm closing fast behind her. Chi just seemed as fragile, as vulnerable, and yet a survivor. She had come here for a better life and my son was treating her to fish and chips. In a way I was proud of him. He had a generosity of heart that didn't come from his bourgeois upbringing. Three days ago I wouldn't have recognised it.

Mark gulped down his last chip, licked his fingers and threw the polystyrene tray in the bin next to the bench. 'Thanks for that. I was starved. Sorry I didn't have any cash, Dad's lost his wallet.'

'That is OK. I work, I have money. You are a pauper,' Chi giggled.

My lofty ideas about my son's generosity took a

nosedive.

'Your English is so good. Have you lived here long?'

'No, not long. Just under a year. Work experience. But I studied English in Vietnam. My family had this plan for me: they wanted me to leave Vietnam behind and go to live in America. Easy life: chewing gum, driving big cars.'

'I'm glad you came here instead. We have treacle tart and double-decker buses. The weather may be crap, but we carry on regardless. It's really a very homely place, though – if you're an outdoor kinda girl – and our outstanding pubs deserve a mention.'

They were grinning at each other, the stupid sort of grins of two people who find everything hilarious because they are plain happy. Chi managed to finish her chips and they decided to take a walk along the quayside. He was tall and gangly; she was dainty and supple. She could probably walk between his legs with her head held high if the fancy took her.

'I am just passing here,' she said suddenly. 'My work experience is up next month. I am going home.'

Mark was taken aback. For him it had only just begun. I felt for him. Still, this was only a little adventure. It was a shame it couldn't last, but it would be safer for him if it ended sooner rather than later. This way he stood a better chance of not being found out. Charlotte was an astute girl and she would stand up for herself. She had the upper hand after all: she was wearing his ring even if – for now – he chose to forget it.

'You could get a job here.'

'Yes, I could, but I want to go home.'

'Surely you don't?'

'You think Vietnam is not good enough?'

'I didn't mean it that way.'

'But you are right: Vietnam is a sad place, very poor. We still live in houses on stilts and eat rice three times a day … But it is my home.'

'We have this saying in England: your home is where your heart is.'

'That is a wise saying. Vietnam is my home. That is where my heart is,' Chi put her small hand, palm down, on her small chest. 'When I completed my English degree, I really wanted to please my father, but I could not bring myself to go to America. I took up medicine. I can do a lot of good being a doctor in Vietnam. More good than being a doctor anywhere else.'

'How much time have I got?'

'To seduce me?'

'Yes, to win you over.'

'Two weeks.'

'That will have to do.' I had never seen Mark look so determined. 'Can I start straight away? Can I kiss you now?'

The girl laughed: 'I have been warned against European men!'

'You've got to give me a chance.' Mark was dead serious. He picked her up like a feather and carried her to the nearest bench. He stood her on it so that they faced each other and kissed.

The rotten siren was back in my house. She was made up from head to toe, dripping with golden Max Factor foundation and oozing poisonous scents. Her face was like a spearhead: sharp and bony. Her cheekbones cut through the skin. Her lips pouted. She entered without ringing the bell, for which I couldn't blame her considering that the front door stood ajar. Rob was having bread and cheese; he had long given up on trying to achieve cheese on toast. The grill was still on; hellish red heat was working its way through the fireproof glass door. Soon it would shatter and the stove would explode. The cat was cowering under the kitchen table, looking deeply troubled. Apparently animals can instinctively foretell natural disasters long before they

107

occur. Rob's cooking was a natural disaster of catastrophic proportions in the making.

Paula waltzed in. The cat took one look at her, and scarpered. Clearly, Paula was more of a threat to him than the house going up in smoke. I smiled under my breath and for the first time in God-knows-how-long I thought of the furry creature with genuine affection. He knew a devil when he saw one.

She frowned at the cat and headed straight for the cooker. With a flourish she flicked the grill off. 'Burning the house down, darling Rob?' She threw the key to the Mini on the table. 'I borrowed your car. Hope you don't mind. There is a tiny dent in the passenger door. This bastard four-wheel-drive parked *so* close, I couldn't get out of my space without taking his indicator with me.' She kissed Rob on the cheek. Both Rob and I recoiled.

'How did you get in, Paula?'

'The door was open, darling Rob.' With a sigh she plonked herself on a chair, arched her back, and volleyed her tennis-ball tits at him. They levelled with his eyes, and hovered, defying gravity. I wished they dropped, just dropped from her chest.

Rob gestured towards his plate, 'Would you like some … something to eat?'

'A glass of wine'd go down well, darling Rob.' She knew where to find the next bottle. She uncorked it expertly and poured two glasses. 'Shall we sit in the lounge? Put our feet up? These chairs are so damn uncomfortable.' She clearly had dishonourable intentions: she went around the house, snooping, asking if the children were home. Rob was ill at ease with her next to him on the couch, side-twisted like a mermaid, bony knees digging into his left thigh in an attempt to tunnel through to his groin. I knew he was impervious to her charms. The woman was delusional. She ran her fingertips down from his lips, across his chest and to his belt buckle with a confident familiarity which unnerved me and Rob. I wished he had the guts to send her packing. Instead, he emptied half of his wine glass in one go. Not a good sign.

'I spoke to that Polish doctor today,' she said. 'I take it you know the prognosis?'

'Yes, I do,' he sounded hollow.

'I'm sorry, Rob darling,' she threw her arms around his neck and gazed into his eyes with an expression that could easily pass for earnest concern if you didn't know she was a trained actress. 'Believe me, I am sorry.' Rob remained unresponsive so she let go of his neck and took hold of his hands instead. 'But just remember I am here for you now. For you and the kids.'

'Thank you, Paula. It's kind of you.' Rob finished off his wine and smiled at her faintly, his lips burgundy red. Was he really buying it? The witch was creeping into our life like poison ivy – a blind man would see it with his eyes closed!

'I am here and I won't go away. Not this time,' she assured him. 'I've never stopped thinking of us. We've always been meant for each other. You were my first. All I wanted was to celebrate us and all I could do was to keep quiet. It hurt, it hurt like hell! When I saw you at the wedding, I didn't know whether to cry or to laugh … Of course, I wouldn't ruin your wedding day – it's just not me! And of course it was hard to walk away and take our secret with me …' She lowered her gaze and adopted a pensive expression. 'Our bitter-sweet secret – I took it away, nourished it, pampered it, loved it for both of us … All those years … I stayed away, gave you a chance to forget me. But I am back. Here for you. Here to stay.'

What the hell was she raving on about? Was this part of one of her entirely fictional performances or was there, hiding in the recesses of her madness, some truth to it?

'Paula, it's OK. I'm OK.'

'No, you're not. You're in denial. I know the

symptoms, I've been there. You go around building up your little life, from scratch, brick by brick putting a wall around your true feelings. But they are there, ready to break free.' She kissed him, this time on the lips, and he let her. 'Just like our first time, remember?'

'Well ... It was –'

Well, what?!

She wouldn't let him finish a sentence. She crossed his lips with her finger, and went on with her monologue peppered with a bit of chuckle and a touch of poise. 'I will never forget your face when you saw me at the wedding? You were ... what's the word? Ah, yes! You were *transfixed*. Did you feel the same way I did – that lightheaded sensation when all the blood drains from your brain? That exhilaration! That utter loss of control!'

Oh, yes! That one joint too many!

'It was a surprise.' Rob – the master of understatement!

'It was *destiny* that we should meet again!' Paula – the mistress of exaggeration! 'How we craved each other! How we were drawn towards the inevitable!'

If I had my body on me at this very moment, if my blood was circulating in my spectral veins, it would've drained all the way to the floor. Paula and Rob! Was I really in a coma, doing the *Big Brother* watch over my husband and sister, or was this a dream? A bad, bad dream, but I would wake up from it to find myself alive and well next to my snoring husband.

'It was instant, wasn't it? We found each other just like that,' she clicked her fingers. 'Remember how it felt?'

'I was surprised,' Rob repeated haplessly. 'I was surprised you were Georgie's sister. It was too much of a shock ...'

'You wanted me then, just like the first time, that New Year's Eve's night. Damned wedding! Damned Georgie! Always in the way! But you can have me now and no one shall stop us. Take me! Take me as I am!' She threw her head back, eyes shut. Nothing happened so she opened one eye and assessed Rob's paralysed form, impotent, incapable of action. She rose like a phoenix and flew at him with revived energy – striking while the iron was hot. She intoned, 'Now we can go back in time, Rob darling. There's nothing – no one – standing in our way. It was worth waiting for …' It was the second time that day that someone had referred to me as *out of the way*. A thought had crossed my mind that they had all been conspiring to get rid of me.

Rob stared at her. 'Paula?'

'Yes, darling?'

'It was only a one-night stand we shared when we were very, very drunk. We were both way too young; we thought that's how it was done. We didn't know any better. But that doesn't change the fact that we were – and are – total strangers. Plus, I am a married man. Even if I wanted to, which I –'

'You don't have to pretend in front of me. Please don't …' She was cold, serious. This really sounded like a cry for help, like the 'Please save me!' she had never uttered to the right audience.

Rob shook off her slight frame and got up from the couch. I sighed with relief. Honestly, for a minute there, he had me worried. 'Paula, I'm not pretending anything. Let me take you home.'

'Don't tell me you forgot,' irritation was rising in her voice like fog.

'I didn't forget, Paula. Of course, I didn't. You were the first girl I had sex with, but it was … Well, it didn't mean … ' he was struggling to find the correct words: words that would say it as it was without hurting my poor sister's feelings. 'Well, my marriage to Georgie superseded whatever we may have had … I mean, it was a one-off. I love Georgie. She's my wife … You are her sister.'

Warm, red blood was again pumping through my ectoplasmic arteries and I felt alive, more alive than I had been in years. But it didn't last. Paula triumphed in the end.

'But does she love you? Has she ever? Did she care about being your wife when she was fucking Tony?'

'Tony?'

'Tony Sebastian, our ... how shall I put it? Our mutual friend: Georgie's and mine. He and I – we don't keep any secrets from each other. He told me all about it. A sordid affair if I ever had one myself! They were at it for months fucking like rabbits behind your back. Sorry I had to break it to you like that, but I hate the idea of the husband always being the last one to find out.'

This was the point, the point where I saw Rob's face, the point where I wished I was *really* dead.

Rob dropped Paula off at her flat without a word. I don't think he meant to be rude – he just couldn't say anything. He was stuck for words. As he reversed, he hit something with the side of his door. Another car – a big four-wheel drive. Its right indicator went crashing to the ground. I noticed that the left one was already smashed. An alarm went off, but Rob drove away without stopping. He didn't hear it.

I sat next to him silently. I wanted to tell him that Tony and I was a one-off, just like Paula and him. I wanted to tell him our marriage meant more to me than anything because I loved him too and I *was* his wife. But the words didn't come. My words were stuck, too.

He drove like a lunatic and missed a couple of red lights. I didn't know where we were going. We were in an unfamiliar suburb when he finally stopped and turned off the engine. A woman came out from a house beyond a low hedge. Leaving his key in the car, Rob ran towards her. She was the chorizo-fingered Mother Earth from work,

Olivia.

'You said I could come and talk to you any time …' He was frantic.

'Yes, come in. You look … terrible!' Her baby-blue eyes were unbelievably rounded.

Inside, they didn't talk. Not really. He only told her he had to be close to her or he would go mad. He cried. She held him. There was so much hunger and need in the way he reciprocated her embrace that it stunned me. I didn't think they would ever let each other go.

'Can I stay with you tonight?' Rob asked Olivia, and she nodded. She took him to her bed upstairs. A fat tabby cat was lying on the bed. It hardly acknowledged their arrival. She undressed Rob and took her own clothes off – all of them, down to the sensible knickers. I got a glimpse of her pubes just before she slid under the duvet, next to him. She was a natural blonde. Everything was natural about her: her breasts were full to the point of bursting, but not grotesquely round the way silicon would shape them; there were bulges of fat on her stomach, free-flowing and gelatinous in a puddingy sort of way. She would be considered yummy by some men. Was that how Rob saw her? I couldn't tell. He was in no state to appreciate her nakedness, and she didn't offer it to him. They were lying together innocently until he stopped sobbing. She stroked his hair for a while and then fell asleep, too.

It was the first night since my accident that I could not curl up next to my snoring husband. Three would be a crowd.

I had some unfinished business with Paula. From the perspective of time I don't know what I was hoping to achieve by going back to her place. I couldn't haunt her – only her conscience could do that and she didn't have one. I couldn't confront her – she would've welcomed a chance to flaunt her theatrical superiority by delivering the final

113

punchline. And she would've found a way of blaming me. After all, I *had* been bonking Tony like a mad rabbit. That much was true. Bizarrely, that may have been the first thing Paula didn't have to fabricate in order to destroy me.

In a strange twist of fate, I didn't find her celebrating. She was slumped on the floor amongst the piles of old family photographs – the ones with me and Rob, Mother and Dad, all sporting moustaches and round spectacles Paula had drawn for her personal entertainment.

Her pose was that of a rag doll: legs stretched wide apart, one shoe on, one shoe off; back bowed, head hanging down, every body part seemingly disjointed. She was holding a large pair of florist's scissors, or rather secateurs, and for a moment, instinctively, I felt that pang of anxiety that she was going to hurt herself – stab herself with those bloody scissors. But soon I realised my mistake. She wasn't going to harm herself, not before she had finally disposed of every memory of me and everyone else she cared about. So there she was: on the floor, like a twisted alter ego of Edward Scissorhands, shredding those photographs, cutting across our faces and torsos, decapitating us, amputating our legs and arms. Snippets of glossy paper tumbled from under her fingers. And she was wailing. Sobs shook her small, wretched body like a dog would shake a rag doll. The rag doll that Paula was.

'No one's in the house, wait!' Emma sprang out of the front door and ran towards the battered old Kia. Brandon had just started the engine. 'Wait!'

He smiled at her and wound down the window. His face bore traces of a flour explosion: it was in his eyebrows and his hair, making him look like a Santa apprentice. 'You don't want to kiss me in this state?'

'No one's in the house. Even the dodgy aunt's gone. I don't want to be alone. Can I come with you?'

'No, Emma. I promised your father I'd bring you back

tonight.'

'And you did, but Dad isn't here. Do you really think he'd notice if I was here or not?'

'Don't be stupid, Em. Of course he would. He's a decent bloke.'

'But he isn't here!'

Brandon killed the engine and stepped out of the car. He didn't bother locking the door. 'I'll wait with you until he comes back, all right? Do you think he'd mind if I had a shower? It feels like I've got flour in the crack of my arse.'

With a small towel wrapped around his hips and his skin sweating droplets of water, Brandon was back to his Adonis self. Emma dried his hair with another towel. Wet wisps fell on his forehead. She kissed it, ruffled his hair, and kissed it again. She did all the things I used to do to her when she was a small child: I'd always towel-dry her short curls, kiss her forehead, ruffle the hair so it would fall back into its old, familiar places – a few locks over the eyes, longer streaks to the back of the head, and I would kiss it again, inhaling the clean smell of Johnson's baby shampoo. Now, Emma was doing it to this Brandon creature. She was even sniffing his hair. Did she love him as much I loved her? Was she capable yet – at this tender age – of loving, or was she just reliving a ritual which she knew should mean love? Or, perhaps, she was simply getting what she wanted – *veni, vidi, vici* – getting it her way. And her way she would get it! I could see the first signs of surrender on his part. He has already capitulated, realising all resistance would be futile. What else could a red-blooded twenty-two-year-old do?

They were in Emma's girly-Goth bedroom with its fluffy cushions bearing skulls with bleeding eyeholes, pictures of cats in thick black frames like obituaries, and a bed with a crumpled duvet the colour of menstrual blood. Brandon was sitting on the bed and Emma stood over him, drying and kissing his hair. He put his arms around her hips and drew her close so that his face was pressed against her tummy. His voice was muffled, as if coming from a drum, when he said, 'It's such a good feeling to be home.'

'This home? My home?' Emma asked.

'Any home – just home. That dump where I kip – that's not home. That's just a crap bedsitter, that's what it is … It feels like ages since I was home.'

'Don't you ever go back home? Like, to visit your family and all?'

'There's no home in Chester anymore. They lost it when they divorced. They don't even live in the same city. Since I was thirteen they played this ping-pong with me: three days at Mum's, two days at Dad's. Then she remarried – new daddy couldn't stand the sight of me. And old daddy emigrated to Canada. No more ping-pong – no one wanted me, not even for three days. He paid for my uni, just to keep me put, so I wouldn't follow him. Whatever! I don't give a shit.'

Emma bent over him and lowered her face into his hair. She whispered, 'That doesn't matter. We'll have our home here.'

He lifted his head, 'What, here? In your bedroom?'

'No, not in my bedroom! You're pulling my leg! Again!' She pushed him onto the bed. He went into a freefall, his arms wide opened, laughing. Emma shouted: 'Here – where we are! Wherever we are, silly!'

When I saw the towel unravelling from his hips and revealing the magnitude of his erection, I knew there was no going back. Neither the depth of their conversation nor his traumatic memories of a family breakup had stopped the flow of blood to his manhood. Men are like that; I knew it and Emma would soon find out: their brains are detached from their dicks. *They* have a life of their own.

Brandon pulled her to him and she lay next to him on

her blood-red bed.

'Let's do it now,' my silly daughter said.

They were facing each other; he was scrutinising her, thinking. 'What? Without the virgin white sheets?' There was excitement in his eyes: he had made up his mind to do it.

'Sod the sheets.'

He was undoing the buttons of her shirt from the top and she from the bottom. She lifted her arms so that he could slide the shirt and her bra off her. She became more impassive. Her fingers dug into the fabric of the duvet.

'You're not sixteen yet …'

'What difference do a few days make? I want to do it. Let's do it!'

Vici!

I thought I ought to want to stop them. But I didn't. I was watching, and even that alone felt wrong. I shouldn't be here. This was their life, not mine; their memory, that only they could share. And here I was, gawping.

'I'll try,' he was struggling with her skirt's zip. 'I never told you, and maybe I shouldn't be telling you, but this is my first time, too.'

I decided this would be a good time to visit Mother and her stale biscuit.

I was almost disappointed to see the biscuit gone, with only a few crumbs remaining on the plate by her bedside table. I had become used to that biscuit. Another surprise was Mother: she was in bed, sleeping. She was wearing a net cap on her head, all her hair tucked neatly under it. It came back to me how she would always wear that cap even when Paula and I were girls, except back then she would have rollers like green caterpillars in her hair. Her hands lay demurely on top of the sheets. Her mind was busily at work: she was dreaming. It was quite a discovery to find out that in the dimmest depths of dementia people's brains still ticked away with great determination, even if

117

the mechanism was outwardly shot.

In her dream Mother was about the same age as when she had seduced Dad, perhaps a little younger: her hair was shorter and bouncier, her step too was bouncier, the spark in her eye was still tomboyish and full of the same vigour as in those days when she climbed trees and dived head first into shallow brooks. She was at work, slaving away at her desk, making phone calls, and jotting down notes, which she would put inside brown manila folders bearing case numbers written in ink over a rubber stamp imprint. The folders were piled up on her desk in a neat column. She was the only woman in a large office bustling with the activity of background police work. Yet she didn't look out of place. She was a girl who had been born to be a man, and was hell-bent on living her life accordingly. I had often wondered what made her give up that life; Dad somehow didn't seem big enough to fill the vacuum, but then perhaps people – women – loved differently in those days. They were prepared to self-sacrifice in order to cook, hoover, change bedsheets, and darn socks.

A plain-clothes policeman of a respectable age and with a very good tailor stopped at Mother's desk. He leaned on it heavily, his face levelled with Mother's. Mother held his gaze. 'Sir?'

'It may be your lucky day, Philips. I need a woman to interview a potential witness. It's a delicate matter. I can't call the woman into the station – she's already given her account with her solicitor present, you see? You will have to go and see her under a pretext: a minor, unrelated detail. An unofficial visit – just you. Have a nice, friendly chat with her. Gloria Rilke –'

They'd never get away with it these days. Mother's face nearly broke into a grin, but she managed to restrain herself by biting her lower lip. 'Rilke's case, sir?' she said.

'Yes. She's his only alibi but he's treading on shaky

ground. I know she's hiding something, but she's also having doubts,' he tapped the side of his nose. 'I want you to probe her a bit, see what you can get. No direct questions, just a girlie heart-to-heart. Any discrepancies you can find, understand? Here's the file.' He threw another manila folder on Mother's desk.

'I've read it, sir, cover to cover!' She was trying to keep her voice as low as possible, which sounded rather comical, like she had a speech impairment.

'That's my girl! Go and get her! This'll be your break into real detective work – if you do it right.'

In her dream – in her glorious recollection – Mother said, 'Sir!', and at last let that eager grin flash across her face, but in her bed she was scowling. And she was fighting the memory. I could tell by how her body stiffened and she shook her head, mumbling a distorted '*No*'.

To no avail. She was in an empty house. The lights were off. She was feeling her way along a dark corridor. 'Mrs Rilke? Mrs Rilke!' There was a shuffling and a muffled noise at the end of the passage, perhaps in the room with an open door. 'Mrs Rilke? My name is Celia Philips, Sergeant Celia Philips.' Deliberately, Mother omitted that little qualifying *W* for woman before her rank of police sergeant. She would've considered it a slight every time she heard it. In her job, the fact that she was a woman was neither here nor there. It was a man's job that she was doing, and yet she knew she was better at it than any man. Why split hairs over gender?

She banged on the door with her fist – man-like. 'May I have a word? Are you there?'

A figure: slim, tall, dark – dark and blurred like everything else in that black tunnel – burst out of that room. It pushed by Mother; she tripped but found support against the open door. She glimpsed inside the room. A red light from neon across the street illuminated the body of a woman sprawled across a double bed, staring back at her with dead eyes. Mother forced herself to breathe; the figure shot out of the back door.

'Stop! Police!' Mother shouted, and took after the man.

She ran across the kitchen, into the utility room, bumping into the barrelled body of a washing machine. Out in the back garden, she was pushing white sheets that were drying on the line away from her face. She couldn't see the man anymore, but there was a gate, and it was swaying. She dived into the narrow lane behind it. A hundred yards or so away someone had run into metal bins; they tumbled to the ground; someone swore. She followed the clanking noises.

In her dream, she was twisting and, like a mute, trying to utter sounds that would not be said. I wished she would wake up, for her sake, but the memory wouldn't have it. It went on. She was at the back of a busy and noisy place – a dance club perhaps. A slim shaft of light saturated with cigarette smoke streamed out of a slightly ajar back door. Mother seemed to have lost her prey. Panting hard, she scanned the concreted yard.

'Looking for me?' A voice came from a black corner, swiftly followed by the looming bulk of a man. He had no face – it was obscured by the night. Two others were with him; one tall and slim, just like the one she had been pursuing, but she wouldn't be able to swear to it. The dark kept them all faceless.

Mother recoiled. She took a few steps back into the arms of someone behind her.

'A nice little birdie looking for action?'

'One at a time, boys, one at a time …'

Mother was going berserk in her bed. She threw off her sheets; she was kicking hard, mumbling, dribbling from her toothless mouth. The dream was cut into pieces, but I could still see the highlights: two men holding her pinned down, and the other one … one at a time.

At last, mercifully, Mother woke up. The horror – for one split second – registered in her eyes, and then she went blank. She tried to pull her duvet back over her shivering body, but it kept slipping. She reached for her cardigan, which was on the back of a chair by her bed. Her fingers got hold of it; she yanked it off the chair and, as best as she could, covered her lower body with it, pressing with both hands against her stomach. She closed her eyes. There was nothing there. The dream was gone.

I felt bad I had found out. Nobody was supposed to know about it. Dad wasn't supposed to know – he was to think she was a virgin when they did it for the first time, a few months after the rape. The least I could do was to stay with her, keep her warm – if only in her mind.

THE SENTENCE …

Meekly, Mother submitted to the carer, who pulled her beige tights over her knees and clad her in a skirt and the immortal – though badly crumpled – cardigan, over her flimsy nightgown. It clearly expedited matters at bedtime.

'Having a visitor, Celia.' The carer peered into Mother's eyes. 'It's a man! We'll have to get you nice and tidy, won't we?' The woman was short but brawny. Her ankles were swollen, growing out of her shoes like rising dough. 'Shall I comb your hair? Looks like you've been through a hedge backwards!' She took a brush from the bedside table and went for Mother's locks.

Mother blinked rapidly as soon as the brush made contact with her scalp. She tried to wave the carer off, swiping blindly over her head. 'Go away! Away!'

'Go on, Celia, don't be a baby. It won't be long …' The brush turned against the back of Mother's head. There was a knot there: a dry lump of greyness. 'What do we have here?'

Mother was stronger than I imagined, stronger than her carer expected. With one powerful ram of her elbow into the woman's side, she managed to make her double up in pain. 'Go away! Don't touch me!'

'Bloody hell, Celia,' the carer groaned, massaging her left kidney.

Mother glared at her, her fists clenched, menace in her eye. Suddenly, she shut her eyes and screamed. It was a piercing sound that could shatter glass. The door swung open. Rob stood in it, gaping.

'Everything all right?'

The carer thrust the brush into his hand. 'Her hair wants combing. You try it. She's a bloody pain if you ask me!' she told him, and abruptly left him in the room, alone with

Mother. And with the brush.

'Celia?'

Mother opened her eyes and swallowed the scream. She stared at Rob and at the brush in his hand. There was a severe warning in her eyes. Rob got the message. Slowly he walked to the window and deposited the brush on the windowsill. Until that point – until the point of parting with the brush – Mother watched his every step; then her eyes glazed over and remained fixed on the view outside the window. I was used to that; Rob wasn't.

'Celia? Do you recognise me? It's Rob. Georgie's husband. Remember?'

The view outside still had more to offer; Mother gazed serenely, as if the incident with the brush had never happened. Rob looked lost. He probably regretted coming here. Actually I wondered why he had.

'I … Well … It's about … I thought you should know, Celia,' his eyes followed hers towards the window, and outside. It seemed he found it easier to talk to the view than to Mother. 'It's about Georgie – you shouldn't expect her to visit this Tuesday. Maybe not for a while yet. It may be a while, definitely a while … She's not well. She's in hospital.' Mother's lower lip began to tremble. It was her usual routine, but Rob didn't know about that. 'No, she's not ill. Not that way,' he assured her.

Mother muttered something inaudible.

'She is … convalescing. It was an accident, you see? Hit and run. I thought I should let you know in case you were wondering.' It was slowly becoming obvious to Rob that Mother hadn't been wondering – that she couldn't have been doing something as demanding as wondering. He tore his eyes away from the window and looked at Mother briefly, somehow relieved she had taken it so well. He bent over her and whispered into her ear, 'You're so lucky, Celia …' He squeezed her hand. 'I'd better be going, then. I'll visit, I'll try.'

He got up. Our wedding picture, propped on a shelf, caught his eye. He picked it up, touched it. His finger picked up some dust and left behind a curved line which revealed both our faces with greater clarity. 'I may have to make a decision about Georgie I don't want to make. I want her to live, but not like that. Do you understand? I hope you do, Celia. Georgie wouldn't have wanted –'

'Georgie would have been better off being a boy.' Mother wasn't looking at him, but her words were clear. There was an eerie lucidity in them that contrasted with her blank face. Rob stared, dumbstruck.

'When she was born – a girl – I cried. I was so disappointed. Not for me – for her. A girl … a girl … poor thing …' Mother's voice trailed off. It sounded frail, wailing. 'But it isn't her fault. She didn't ask for it.' She looked straight at Rob. 'Georgie's a good girl. Don't hurt her.'

Rob was still staring while Mother had suddenly lost interest in the matter, and turned towards the window. Her lower lip quivered.

'No, I won't. You're right: she didn't ask for it,' Rob said in a low voice. 'Thanks, Celia.' He left.

Mother didn't acknowledge his departure. She was ten again. She was in a wood: thick undergrowth, knee-high ferns. She was frightened. Lost. I could hear her heart beating very fast, and her shallow breathing. Through the low hanging canopy of tree branches she was looking for the sun to guide her out, but the sky was overcast. She was a brave little girl. She told herself she had to keep her hair on and keep going in the same direction. Whichever direction it was, she was bound to reach the end of the forest. It was not boundless. She started walking.

Mark was sleeping on the couch – a sizeable three-seater, yet his thin legs were still too long for it, and were bent over one side of it, dangling lifelessly like the wooden limbs of Pinocchio. Part of his body was elevated so that his head rested high on the back of the couch; the rest of him was convoluted and twisted on the seat. He looked extremely uncomfortable, even for a wooden puppet. Yet he was fast asleep, his head thrown back, his mouth gaping open, producing self-indulgent, contented snores. There was an empty bottle of something – no doubt alcoholic – on a small table by the couch. Two tumblers stood next to it. Other than that the room was immaculately tidy. I should say it was *worryingly* tidy: it was tidier than I would've cared to make it myself, and that was saying something. The girl was either bordering on obsessive-compulsive, or we were talking serious cultural diversity here. She was in the corner of the room, folding bed sheets into neat squares and putting them in a large drawer under a sleeper-sofa. She glanced over her shoulder at my sleeping son. She held him with a steady gaze, listening to his jolly grunts. Once she was sure he was truly immersed in full-blown slumber, she slipped out of her pyjamas (yes, she had been wearing sensible striped PJs). Her body was tiny and perfectly formed; it wasn't toned, like Paula's, but there wasn't an ounce of fat on her – everything was smooth, in clean lines. She was a character from a Hans Christian Andersen fairy tale. You would trust that girl with your life.

She stepped into the shower in a small, windowless en-suite by her room. I scanned her room: there was very little to rest an eye on. The floor was wooden boards, scrubbed to the bare bone. I could find no family snapshots anywhere, but there was one picture propped on the mantelpiece. It depicted an orange-red sky, a black outline of hills, or a forest, and the white silhouettes of trees. Next to it was a statue of a sitting Buddha, or some other Eastern deity. In a square glass, half-filled with water, swam several white daisies: quite a pleasant sight, I liked the idea though I couldn't be too sure if I would ever use it in my lifetime.

Fresh out of the shower, Chi got dressed in a pair of linen trousers and a body-hugging orange top. Her wet hair soaked into it. She glided barefoot across the wooden floor, without making a single sound. A kitchenette was built into her room. She went about boiling the kettle and making coffee. Mark didn't stir throughout the entire procedure even though the kettle whistled and two mugs clanked loudly against each other when she took them out of a cupboard. You would think he was dead …

She took the mugs to the table, put them down, and gently brushed Mark's shoulder with her elfish fingers.

'Wake up,' she chimed in her tiny, five-year-old's voice. Mark twitched, gave out a startled grunt and opened his eyes. 'You drink coffee?' she asked.

'For you I'll drink anything, but it so happens that coffee is my beverage of choice.' He bravely reached for the mug and downed the steaming liquid in one go. I say 'bravely' because I knew for a fact Mark detested coffee; he had been brought up a proper English Breakfast tea devotee. But that didn't matter anymore – he was head over heels in love. It was clear they hadn't had sex yet and at this point he would drink boiling lava to get into the girl's knickers. I wished they had got on with it so he could get his perspective back. As it were, he was far from having any sense at all.

'Chi, I don't think I can let you go,' he said. 'In fact, I know I can't.'

'And I don't think you have a choice,' she smirked, 'my shift starts in an hour. We both have to be going.'

'I don't mean that. I mean – you are *it*. For me, you are *it*. That's it. I'm sunk. I can't let you go. I'd be a fool if I did.'

I never knew my son commanded such flair at expressing emotions. It was certainly the first time I had heard it.

Chi shook her head with mock exasperation. 'You are a stubborn man, Mark Ibsen!'

'When I know what I want – I am. You'll *have to* give in to me.'

'I can't stay here. I am stubborn, too. I don't believe in your queen, I won't pray in your church. I am a communist, you know? I am dangerous, and I am going home.' She picked up their mugs and drifted away to the kitchen. She was washing them under the running tap whilst Mark watched. She dried them and put them in the cupboard. It was as if they had never had that coffee.

'I am going with you.'

'To Vietnam?' Her almond eyes rounded.

'I was always going to Vietnam. It's always been my plan.'

'What do you know? Such a small world! We may even be travelling on the same flight!' Chi laughed – little chiming notes bounced in the air. She was laughing – she was trying to laugh it off – but I sensed she was flattered, and hopeful. She wanted him to go with her, and now she was beginning to believe he would. Was this Mark's destiny moment, I wondered, his own Edinburgh Festival?

'I watch my parents. I don't like what I see, and the thing is, I'm halfway there – halfway to repeating their life. I don't want their life, I want my own! I just didn't quite know how to break it to them. Well, how to break it to Mum ... Dad would've been all right with it, but Mum ... You don't know my mother. I couldn't do it to her. I was planning to leave anyway – just without telling her ... well, in not so many words ... It would've been a gap year, then ... I'd think of what to say next. But now –'

'Now that she can't stop you?' Chi interrupted him. There was an undertone of condemnation in her voice.

'Now that I met you!' Mark approached her and took the tea towel out of her hands. He put it away, cupped her face in his hands and kissed her. He came out for breath, looking childishly elevated. 'Now I know where I'm going with it! That is *it*. *You* are it! I am going with you whether you like it or not. I'll live next door to you if you don't let me in. I'll become a communist!'

They were both laughing: stupidly, loudly, and drunkenly. He was kissing her. She was kissing him. Before I knew it, before I had the presence of mind to get myself out of there, they were tearing each other's clothes off, Mark was lying stark naked on the hard floor with his back arched and his eyes rolled into the back of his head, and his temptress was sat astride him, bouncing up and down like a bunny rabbit. So I stayed, averting my gaze and closing my ears to their impending full Technicolor orgasm. I collapsed in an emotional pile of my own and marvelled at how, until now, I had managed to prevent my son from being his own man and living his own life, without ever realising what a burden I had been for him.

Mark broke it to his father as soon as he got home. Rob had only just got back himself after a night out with the warm-blooded Olivia, followed by a half-decent conversation with my mother. It seemed to me they were all getting on with their lives without me rather well. Rob had just put the kettle on. It was the same kettle he had carried to my side when I was lying on the pavement with my brains pouring out of my nose; the same kettle that had kept me company by my hospital bed until he took it home and lovingly restored it to the kitchen worktop.

'Mark! Just in time for a cup of tea! I've just put the kettle on.'

'Coffee, Dad. I'll have coffee.' Mark sat down at the kitchen table. Rob gazed at him, puzzled about the coffee, but made no comment. Unshaven, dishevelled, and pale, they both looked seriously shagged out, and at least one of them truly was.

'Had a good night out?'

'Yes. Very good. The best night of my life.'

Rob was looking increasingly alarmed. 'How's Charlotte?'

'Charlotte?' It was Mark's turn to look puzzled. It appeared he couldn't recall any person by that name.

'Yes, Charlotte. Are you all right?'

'Yes, like I said, couldn't be better.'

'So, where were we? Charlotte …'

'We got engaged, but I need to talk to you about something-'

'Engaged? Well … congratulations are in order?'

'Dad, I want to talk about something. It's important.'

'Your engagement would be important, wouldn't it? Mum would like that.' Rob attempted a fond smile at the mention of me, but all he managed was a twitch. 'Well, well, engaged … Last night? You got engaged last night?'

'No, no … last night I was with someone else.'

'Riiight …'

'Her name is Chi. It's Vietnamese for a twig. She's Vietnamese and I am in love with her. I'm going to Vietnam. With her.'

'Um.' It was a short statement even by Rob's standards, but I didn't expect much more under the circumstances.

'You know I always wanted to go to the Far East …'

'Um … Yes, for your gap year!'

'Dad, this is it. For me, this is *it*. After the exams, I'm off. I'm going to apply for a job with Amnesty International or the Red Cross, or something or other. Hopefully –'

'Well, it's your life …'

'Dad, I always wanted it – I just didn't know I did. This is my chance to break away from this … this … this vicious cycle! And, like I said, I'm in love and Chi is Vietnamese, which obviously plays a big part in it –'

He was spluttering words. He was drunk on it. Intoxicated with excitement. Had I ever seen my son so out of control? In my perverse way, I was enjoying it. Knowing my boy had blood – not water – flowing through his arteries. *Go, Mark*! I shouted as if all my money was on him. *Go, Mark*!

And then came the anti-climax. Rob said, 'What about Charlotte? Haven't you just got engaged? Or was it to Chi, I get confused …'

'It was to Charlotte, but it was a mistake. I got muddled up, Mum in hospital … just muddled up. She'll get over it when I'm gone.'

'Who will? Mum or Charlotte?'

'Charlotte, of course!' It went without saying that I would never get over it, and they both knew it.

'So you haven't told Charlotte? She doesn't know?'

'Is there a point telling her? It'll only upset her.'

'Don't you think she should know?'

'She will! Once I'm gone she'll realise.'

'She should be told.'

'Do you want to tell her?'

Rob stared. He wasn't one for rocking boats. 'No, I don't. I wouldn't know where to begin.'

'Neither would I. Now you can see my point.'

Rob nodded. They drank in silence. Nothing else was to be said about the matter now that it was all clear and straightforward in their heads. Like father, like son … A thought occurred to me. They could have both spent lifetimes tied up to people they didn't want to be with, unable to bring themselves to get away, unable to hurt anyone's feelings. They could both conform, against their will but in agreement with their conscience, until circumstances released them from their obligations, almost by accident. In Rob and Mark's case it was the accident that had befallen me which could set them free. It wasn't the most pleasant or self-indulgent thought I ever had, but it was the closest I had come to knowing my husband and son.

Brandon shook Emma awake. 'They're downstairs,' he whispered, greatly agitated. 'Your father and your brother! How am I gonna get out? If they know I spent the night here …'

Emma smiled at him dreamily. She threw her long, skinny arms around his neck. 'I'm happy,' she told him.

'Em,' he smiled back, and then confessed against his better judgement, 'you're trouble, but I bloody well love you.'

'It was magic. Last night,' she stretched and purred like a fully domesticated black panther, 'our first time was magic …'

'It was …' He lay next to her and she put her head on his chest. 'But I'll have to go home some time,' he sighed.

'Don't worry. They won't come here. No one comes to my room. Except Mum, but Mum …' Emma picked on her nails. She was chewing the cuticle of her forefinger, a tortured grimace on her face. 'I miss Mum, even though she's such a pain in the arse, I wish she was home.' I could swear tears welled in her eyes. I felt defeated by those tears. My daughter, who had never given me a second glance, a second thought, a second chance, was wishing me back and I couldn't make her wish come true. What sort of mother was I?

'She'll get better. Believe in it.' Brandon kissed my daughter's forehead. I should be saying that; I should be offering her that kiss. I should be making her feel better.

Emma nodded, but couldn't say a word without letting those tears roll. Her lips were pressed together tightly.

'People survive accidents.'

'Yes, I know. And it's only a bump on the head …'

Plus a botched CPR! A cardiac arrest! Vegetative state …

The doorbell rang. Brandon cursed under his breath. 'Who the hell is that?' With shaky fingers he was doing up his jeans.

134

'I'll see who it is. It's probably my fake auntie. She's been all over Dad since Mum's gone off sick.' Emma put her finger on Brandon's lips. 'Sit tight, be quiet. I'll be back.'

DS Thackeray looked pleased with himself (if his drawn face with its permanently downturned mouth and heavily hooded eyes could effectively convey any pleasure) when he sat with Rob and Mark in the lounge. Before getting down to business, he went by the book and asked about my wellbeing.

'No improvement, I'm afraid,' Rob told him, looking apologetic for not being able to offer anything more upbeat on the subject. 'Would you like a cup of tea, or anything?'

Tea had seemed to solve most of Rob's problems in the past, but not any more. The policeman shook his head. 'There's been a breakthrough in the investigation. We've identified the man who –'

'Who's that?' Emma was standing in the door. Expecting just Rob and Mark, she was wearing only her dressing gown. It was tied up loosely on her hips; one side was longer than the other. Instinctively, she pulled the lapel over her chest and folded her arms. She shifted on her bare feet defensively and leaned against the door frame.

'This is the policeman investigating the hit-and-run.'

'DS Thackeray.'

'I see. Have you caught him, the man who did it to Mum?'

'We've identified him. Positive identification. The CCTV photo we showed your father was unclear, but we've recovered prints from the stolen car. They belong to Jason Mahon, a car thief, well known to us. There's a definite link between him and your mother. We're looking into that connection – a case, one of the last cases your mother was working on before the incident.'

'Incident?' Emma asked. 'So it's no longer an *accident*?'

She was sharp, my girl. I was proud of her. When push came to shove, she was sharper than Rob and Mark put together. She knew how to tune into the subtleties of language and she was not inhibited by basic politeness, something neither Rob nor Mark could shake off however hard they tried.

'Yes, we believe it was deliberate. We may be looking at attempted murder. Our officers are on their way to Gaolers Road to effect an arrest –'

Emma stiffened. 'To Gaolers Road? What's his name? Your suspect – what's his name again?'

A strange noise came from somewhere outside in the garden. It was as if a sack of potatoes had fallen from a height.

'What was that?' Both Rob and Mark went to the patio door to take a look.

Emma persisted, 'The name … what was that name?'

'Jason Mahon.'

'Jason …' she was pale. They couldn't possibly guess, but I knew she had put two and two together. 'May I see his photo? Do you have his photo? You said CCTV photo …'

Thackeray passed the picture to her. She took it tentatively, slowly, as if afraid of what it may reveal. She gave out a thin gasp when she looked at it. It was fortunate that Rob and Mark were still surveying the garden, because just by looking at her, they would have guessed something was not right. She returned the photo.

'Do you know him?'

'Excuse me, please.' She ran out of the room.

Her bedroom was empty and the window had been left open. Brandon had done a runner. He must have heard everything. Emma stood in the midst of her gothic paraphernalia, lost and small. She was Little Miss Muffet in a haunted house full of spiders.

She retched, covered her mouth, and ran to the toilet. The contents of her stomach poured out of her.

'Emma? Are you all right?' It was Rob's voice.

'Fine, Dad,' she managed to say. 'It must be something I've eaten.' She washed her mouth and her face under the tap. For a long, tortuous moment she stared at her own face in the mirror. The water had made her mascara run. Wet wisps of dyed black hair clung to her cheeks, like cracks in a canvas. My poor girl – she was scared and confused. I could guess how she felt. I would've felt the same way: an accomplice in her own mother's murder. I didn't want her to feel like that. There was no reason to, but even if I could tell her that, she wouldn't have listened. Emma never listened to me and if she did it was only to do the exact opposite of what I was asking her to do. At this very moment, she desperately needed me to assure her that it wasn't her fault so that she could argue with me and insist that it was. It would've made her feel better. But I couldn't say anything.

I watched her. She thoroughly dried her face in a towel, making sure that every bit of make-up was erased from her skin. Without the eyeliner, her eyes looked smaller and rounder, like a child's eyes. She brushed her hair and put it into a ponytail. In her room she changed into leggings and a white T-shirt. I didn't know she even had a single item of white clothing. The paleness of her skin blended with the whiteness of the T-shirt.

From the bathroom cupboard she fetched a black rubbish bag and into it went her entire gothic world: the posters from the walls, the blood-red bed sheets, the trinkets and makeup from the dressing table, and most of the contents of her wardrobe. She dragged the bulging bag down the stairs. DS Thackeray was gone. Mark was gone. Rob was getting himself into his gardening boots, the ones without laces and with mud-caked, falling-off soles.

'What's that?' He pointed to the black bag.

'Nothing. Just rubbish.'

'You've been tidying up?' He smiled, grateful for her efforts.

She dropped the bag in the middle of the hallway. The veneer of her cold composure suddenly melted away, leaving behind a skinny little girl choking on tears. 'Dad?'

Rob, already equipped with a trowel, gazed at her. 'Emma? Are you not well? Is it something you ate? I've heard you throwing up …'

'No … No … It's my fault Mum's in hospital!'

He charged towards her, trowel in hand, gardening boots leaving a trail of mud on the carpet. He tried to hug her, but the rubbish bag stood between them like a beacon of restraint. 'Of course, it isn't your fault. You must never blame yourself. Your mum's accident was just that … an accident.'

'He was trying to kill her!'

'We don't know that! The police are only guessing. We don't know that lad; we don't know what he was trying-'

'Jason! His name is Jason. He's Brandon's flatmate! Brandon knew! Jason does anything Brandon tells him … Brandon is like a god to him …'

'Who's Brandon?'

Emma looked at Rob, disbelieving. For a moment, I was sure, she would give up, shrug her shoulders and fall back on her usual '*Whatever!*' But she was a changed girl. 'Brandon, yeah?' she spoke slowly like to an idiot. 'Dad! You met Brandon last night. He's my boyfriend. Was my boyfriend …'

'The fireman?'

'Yes, the bloody fireman!' Emma punched the black rubbish bag to vent her frustration.

'Well … in that case …' Rob was lost for words. 'I mean, are you sure?'

'I want to talk to that copper. I want to tell him.'

'Yes, let's do that. If that makes you feel better … We'll go to the station.' Rob picked up the car keys from the kitchen table and ushered Emma to the Mini. I don't know what it is about Rob and his props, but he took the trowel with him and held it in his right hand as he steered the car. He was still holding on to it while they were sitting at the police station, waiting for DS Thackeray to be found. He was brandishing the thing like a deadly weapon in the face of the riff-raff of detainees swearing their innocence and aggrieved citizens wishing to make a complaint to the officer on duty who happened to be on his tea break away from the desk. Emma and Rob were in for a long wait. Neither of them thought of simply telephoning the man.

It was an hour later when DS Thackeray hurried through the front door, telling off two constables who lagged behind him looking positively brow-beaten. DS Thackeray was flushed deep red. He was thrusting his forefinger into the face of one of his constables just as Rob stood up to greet him, possibly preventing the final onslaught. 'DS Thackeray, hello … Rob Ibsen, you remember?' he began tentatively. 'My daughter has something to report. It may be helpful to your investigation.'

The policeman's pointing finger froze where it was as he turned to Rob. Now, it was in Rob's face. 'Mr Ibsen? Yes! What is it?' he asked impatiently.

Emma got up. She spoke, calm and collected, factual: 'I know Jason. He's flatmates with my boyfriend. My boyfriend was upstairs in the house when you came to tell us about Jason. He must've heard and got out, through the window. My bedroom window is on the first floor. He jumped.'

'He was in your bedroom? What was he doing in your bedroom?' Rob raised his trowel and pointed it at Emma.

One more disjointed move and that trowel would cause someone grievous bodily harm.

'Miss Ibsen ... I see.' Thackeray gazed at her sternly. 'Jason Mahon wasn't home when our men got there to effect arrest. He'd just left, apparently ... The front door was wide open. My men may have passed him in the street as he had just left the house. He knew we were coming. Someone –'

'Brandon must've warned him,' Emma finished the sentence for him.

'Brandon, is your boyfriend, I take it?'

'Was.'

'We'll need his details. You'll have to tell us all you know, no matter how insignificant it may seem to you.'

'It's all bloody significant to me,' Emma muttered under her breath, and she and Rob followed the sergeant to the interview room.

I found it hard to believe poor Brandon had anything to do with this whole nightmare other than to know about it. Jason would have confided in him that day when Emma had found them both arguing. Jason had been blaming Brandon, but I knew it wasn't Brandon who had told Jason to do it. It was Ehler. I knew it. And Tony knew it, too. If there was a shred of doubt in his mind about it, it was dispelled when he received a phone call from my young, pimply usurper, Aitken.

The ringing telephone dragged Tony out of the shower. He took the call, wearing nothing but a sheet of frothing soap. His tight buttocks glistened. A momentary current of pleasure travelled through my ectoplasmic body at the faint, distant memory of our past carnal encounters.

'Tony Sebastian.'

'Hello, Tony! It's Gavin. How are you doing?'

'Gavin?' Tony frowned, his thoughts cross-referencing his mind's address book, wondering who the twit that was calling him this early on a Saturday morning could possibly be.

'Gavin Aitken, Crown Prosecutions.'

'Ah, Gavin, my man! How are you? What's up?'

'Fine, fine ... Just a courtesy call, really. It's about one of Georgiana's cases ... you acted for Michael Ehler. The police want to re-open the case. Expect a visit.'

Tony grabbed a towel and vigorously dried his face and hair. He was now fully awake. 'Why would they be interested in an old case?'

'It's to do with the hit-and-run. They've identified the perpetrator. He was Georgiana's Crown witness in Ehler's case. They think there's a connection.'

'Can't blame them.'

'Well, they're looking into it. I'm wading through the file as we speak. What could be better on a nice Saturday morning? Anyway, thought I'd bring you up to speed.'

'Thanks, Kevin.'

'No problem. It's Gavin, actually.'

Tony parked his virginal white MGA convertible on a double yellow line, the right-side wheels on the pavement, blocking the entire width of it. Above it, towered the sharp ascent to a huge house sprawled on a hill amongst tall, mature trees and thick tufts of bushes. An unassuming iron gate, narrow and blackened, guarded a stone path leading up to the house. Even by Clifton's leafy standards it was a formidable looking residence. Respectable and very private. It belonged to Michael Ehler – or rather to Mr Prickwane of Bedminster, who was probably still getting used to the idea of being a real estate oligarch.

A woman, wearing a black dress with white trimmings, opened the door. 'Good morning, Mr Sebastian. Is Mr Ehler expecting you?' Her clipped enunciation could have rivalled the Duchess of Cornwall's – and her bright-eyed and bushy-tailed appearance could have given the Duchess of Cambridge a run for her money.

'Just tell him I'm here,' Tony said through his teeth.

'Of course.' The blue-blooded maid departed, leaving Tony in a marble-floored reception room which could easily have passed for a *Downton Abbey* filming location.

Within minutes, Ehler appeared wearing a jovial expression on his face and a pair of embroidered slippers on his feet. He was a big, corpulent man with chubby cheeks and a bald head that always reminded me of Winnie the Pooh. The small, pinched nose perched in the middle of his bloated face was trademark Winnie. But that was where the similarities ended. His smile was forced and disingenuous; his forehead glistening with sweat.

'Tony, I half-expected you! I said to Esther, *You know, Esther, I wouldn't be surprised if Tony popped over today*. And here your are!' Ehler opened his arms as if to embrace Tony, but managed only a lukewarm handshake. Tony's manner was rigid. If Ehler noticed it, he didn't let it trouble him. 'Come in! A few things to go over ... We'd best go to my study.' He gave the maid a throwaway glance. 'No one's to disturb us, Mrs Thaw.'

Ehler had a study! A poor panel beater with a study was nothing short of a pope with a condom, and yet there it was. Ehler had led Tony into a panelled room, furnished with a desk, high armchair, a row of filing cabinets, and a mini-bar. One wall displayed a collection of works by prominent English writers and a full set of the *Encyclopaedia Britannica*. In a way, Ehler's place reminded me of Tony's. It was more or less its faithful replica. Both places had an air of the over-the-top bourgeois about them.

The study had a bay window overlooking the back of a mature garden in the full bloom of May. The garden didn't seem to belong to its owner: it was tranquil and natural; free of pretension. Ehler's house must have been prised away from some poor bastard Bristolian intellectual who fell on hard times and had to make way for a panel-beating crime lord charging forth from the fringes of society.

So this was the headquarters of Ehler's empire! This was where he conducted his dirty business, pulled the strings, received petitioners ... There was more to Winnie the Pooh than met the eye!

'Drink?' he offered and slipped into his high armchair, which groaned under his weight. Clearly, he didn't expect Tony to take him up on his offer this early in the day. And Tony didn't. He went to the window, looked out and breathed deeply.

He spoke without turning back to face his client. 'You told me the prosecutor's hit-and-run had nothing to do with you.'

'And it didn't – not directly.'

'You're taking the piss, Mikey?'

Ehler sighed. There was the indulgence of a forgiving Godfather in that sigh. 'Tony, what did you want me to tell you? I just wanted to keep your conscience clean, yeah? Kept you out of it.'

'You had that woman killed.'

'She dead?'

'As good as. Why the fuck did you do it?'

'Let's get it straight, Tony, yeah?' There was a trace of irritation in Ehler's voice. 'You told me, yeah? You told me she was gonna fry my arse, yeah? You knew I had to do something about it! Don't go all innocent on me now. Let's have that drink. It's lunchtime.' He got up, heaved himself to the bar, and poured two glasses of brandy. He downed one and slid the other one across his desk, towards Tony. 'Here! It'll calm your nerves.'

Tony did not touch it. He said, 'I only asked you to sort out your affairs. I didn't ask you to go around murdering people!'

'A small misunderstanding, then. The boy got carried

away. He was just to tap her on the shoulder, put her out of action for a couple of weeks. A broken leg, that sort of thing. Things don't always go to plan. Anyway, I've got it all sorted, Tony, yeah?' Ehler patted Tony on the back.

'What do you mean *sorted*? She's dying. How can you sort that out?' Tony's fists were closed. His lips curled into a snarl I had never seen before. 'You'll bring her back to life? You've got connections *up there*, have you?'

Ehler didn't notice the snarl. He laughed. 'At least your good humour is back! Don't worry, Tony. Leave it to me. Go home.'

'The police know the boy did it. They'll find him and he will lead them to you,' Tony hissed. 'And you know what, Mikey? I'll be glad when it happens.'

'Ah, but then I'd lead them to you,' Ehler sobered up. 'And we can't have that, can we?'

'I don't give a shit.'

'Good thing that I do, then!' Ehler chuckled amiably. 'I'll look after you. The boy won't talk, I'll make sure of that.'

Tony glared hard at him. 'What do you mean?'

'Here goes,' Ehler lowered his voice. 'He got away. He called me an hour ago. The cops came looking for him, but he got away. Someone tipped him off, lucky sod! He's all panicked and that – can't be trusted to keep his gob shut … In short, he's coming to see me tonight. Do you understand? He's coming to see me, but he won't be leaving.' His voice became a whisper when he said: 'I'll deal with him myself. Consider this matter closed, yeah?'

Tony took a while to respond. At first, he stared at Ehler, trying to digest everything he was telling him. Then he asked: 'What time? What time exactly is he coming here?'

'Seven, yeah? On the dot; he knows I can get touchy when people don't keep appointments. Anyways, he got no choice. Where else can he go? He's on the run. The boy needs to disappear. Frankly, I be doing him a favour. Personally. No one else needs to know. Relax, Tony. It's as good as sorted. You can trust me.'

He escorted Tony to the front door with an amiable hand on his back. An insincere, toothy smile cracked his face. They shook hands, though Tony didn't respond to Ehler's cheery 'Take care, mate!'

Tony was placated. Naturally, he wasn't overly chummy when parting company with Ehler, but he had left without fuss. It appeared he felt reassured. I felt nauseous. Whether this tragic ending was by his design or somebody else's, he came out of it a cheap traitor. His back was covered – that's all that mattered to him. The fact that several lives were damaged in the process was neither here nor there. To Tony Sebastian it was merely collateral damage. My love-hate relationship with Tony had become one-sided: now I only hated him.

My contempt for him was such that I could no longer see the physical beauty with which he had charmed me for years. That beauty had peeled off him like a snake's skin. Beneath it, he was a flabby, ageing man with liver spots darkening on his hands and thinning hair. Dorian Gray.

I don't know why I followed him as he drove to his dingy basement club. I guess I wanted to feed my eyes on his ugliness; confirm my superiority.

The club was open. It was one of those places that never closes – always keen to serve its patrons' seediest needs. Sleepy jazzy music seeped from the walls, where invisible speakers were camouflaged under canvases brimming with erotica. Tony headed for the bar and ordered tonic water. He gestured to the barman to lean over the counter. The barman – about thirty, chubby, and clearly gay – smiled, flattered by Tony's attention.

'A boy, calls himself Etienne,' Tony said into the barman's keen ear, 'I want to see him. Tell him I'll make it worth his while. I'll wait there,' he pointed to a secluded table in a corner.

'I haven't seen Etienne in a while. Would anyone else do?' The barman fluttered his eyelashes. 'I'm off in half an hour …'

'Etienne.' Tony replied curtly and walked away.

'I'll see what I can do.' His feelings deeply wounded, the barman shrugged and slid into his pocket the fifty-pound note Tony had left on the counter for him.

I was watching Tony concealed in the red shadows of the club, sipping tonic water, smoking a cigarette – a sad picture of a dirty old man, I thought. Somewhere deep, deep inside me, suppressed and unwanted, languished a great, choking sorrow for him. Was it because I loved him that I couldn't condemn him, and couldn't free myself from him? Whatever he did I was drawn to back him, desperate to understand him. Or was it because we had so much in common, Tony and I? I had just been lucky with my life having gone the way it had: smoothly and conventionally. But, had it been derailed at any point in time, would I have ended up just like him: hardened, unscrupulous, self-serving? Wasn't I a survivor, a fighter who hadn't always played it clean? Hadn't it always been about winning for me, too? After all, I'd never denied it – I was an ungraceful loser.

My self-analysis was interrupted by the arrival of none other than Paula. Surprisingly, no one but I was aware of her arrival, though it was quite a dramatic entrance even by Paula's standards. But then she didn't exactly enter the scene in person …

She swooped on me like a big raven or rook, covered in blood. Her hair was dripping wet, clinging to her naked skeletal body. The blood was caked in her hair, smudged across her face like warpaint, and lazily coagulating on her fingertips.

'Georgie!' she demanded, her eyes rounded with disbelief, 'you have to come! Please! You have to save me!'

She dragged me to her flat and there she was – the physical she – peacefully dead in her bathtub. I couldn't believe how she was still trying to steal my thunder! I was supposed to be dying, but hey, she had to beat me to it!

The bathwater was still warm and still crackling with bubbles. Another realisation hit me: Paula had run a scented bubble bath for herself before she got in and cut her wrists! That's what some would call *dying with style*! I had to give it to her – she was good!

The water and even the bubbles were dyed red. Paula's knees were propped up and her head rested comfortably, so only the amount of blood and the fact that she wasn't breathing indicated the woman was dead. A razor had slipped out of her hand and was floating aimlessly in the bath alongside a sponge and a rubber duck with a stupid grin. The cuts on her wrists were deep, ploughed across old scars: old, unsuccessful attempts she had made on her life. Only this time no one had come to save her.

'Georgie? Do something! Call someone!' The ghost of my sister was pulling at my virtual sleeve. I was staring, rather speechless. She was panicking; running around me in circles like a crazed dog. 'I left a message for Rob … He didn't come! Get Rob! He'll come, for you. It's not too late!'

She was dead. It was too late. Rob never read his text messages. He was technology averse. I didn't have the heart to tell her that, but she had fucked it up – irreversibly. There was no getting out of this hole. I was staring at my sister's slashed body. She had done it to herself.

She could've had a life, a life as good as mine had been – simple, traditional – but somewhere something had gone wrong for her. Conversely, it occurred to me, I could've ended up like her: tragic and pathetic, but somewhere, somehow I had been spared. Pure chance. Life was pure chance in a silly old game of Russian roulette. If I had lived it merrily until the day I died from old age I would've never realised that. I would've thought I had earned my life, I had made it what it was through my own strength of character and good planning. I would've died a happy, supercilious twat. At least now I was dying with no illusions. Paula, on the other hand, still believed in Santa Claus and still hoped for a miracle which would present her with yet another chance.

'Georgie,' she was prodding me, her agitation reaching new heights, 'I didn't mean to do that!' She pointed to her earthly remains in the bath. 'You know it! You must help me. You're my big sister, for God's sake! Do something! I don't want to die!'

'But you are dead,' I finally said out loud what I had been thinking quietly all along.

'But …' She paused and gaped at the carnage. I think she was beginning to realise there was no arguing with simple facts. 'But look at this mess! It's awful!' At last she mustered an ounce of self-criticism.

'Let's face it: you've never been particularly tidy. Who said your death – if self-inflicted – would be any tidier than your life.'

'You're such a bitch!' she hissed.

I was used to invectives from Paula. Since we were little girls, Paula would blame me for all her misfortunes and evil deeds. Like that Nativity in which she'd been cast as a donkey. She convinced the world it was my fault because I had been given the part of a camel.

'If Georgia wasn't a stupid camel, I could be Mary, but no, she has to be a camel, and we're sisters! How can a sister of a camel be Mary? It's her fault I'm a donkey!' There was some logic to it, everyone had to admit. She cried and cried. Mother and Dad clucked sympathetically. I felt like such a shit sister. I wasn't worthy to be a speck of dust on her sandals, never mind a bloody camel! The whole household was in mourning.

But that was in the past. Now, it was different. We were both dead, kind of, and by all accounts should be in mourning, but I couldn't be arsed. I shrugged off Paula's criticism with indifference. I didn't even care to ask her why she did it. She had been heading towards this spectacular conclusion all her life. It was inevitable.

I saw little point in hanging about in Paula's flat. I found the mess difficult to handle. Something drew me back to Tony. Perhaps I wanted to witness his final humiliation: the boy turning him down, his ego beaten like a dog. Or perhaps, again, I had this irresistible compulsion to be near him. Fatal attraction at its most pathetic! I was torn between despising and worshipping him, and I couldn't tell which way the winds were blowing in my poor head. Be that as it may, I went back to the club.

Paula tagged along. She didn't want to stay alone in her flat. She had always been a bit of a drag, and that was another thing I'd been quite used to since we were young. Sooner or later I would have to make some decisions: either stay up here in this never-world with my little sister tagging behind me into eternity, or go back to life, disguised as a vegetable. Neither option was too appealing. I pushed decision time out of my mind.

'Are you in love with him?' Paula asked me as soon as we got back to the club and found Tony stooped over his second tonic water, alone and waiting for the boy. To my surprise, his loneliness gave me little satisfaction. I suppose pity could be more gratifying than revenge, and pity is what I felt when I looked at him.

'No! Of course, not. What gave you that idea?' I glared at her, unnerved by her presence and by her bloody unwelcome insightfulness.

'It wasn't long ago when you and he were lovers. I know – he told me.'

'I know you know. I know you told Rob. I know what you were trying to achieve. So, was it worth it?'

We looked at each other. I felt no resentment towards her. In a way I was grateful for what she did. I had discovered things about Rob that would help me let him go – if I had to. I'd found out he could, after all, live without me. Thanks to Paula. Perhaps her telling Rob about my affair was like my own belated confession to him. Perhaps his seeking solace in Olivia was the absolution he had given me. We were quits.

'I'm sorry,' Paula said. It wasn't an act. She genuinely regretted it. She was genuinely seeking absolution for her sins. Probably she was scoring her first brownie points with St Peter. How would that interview at Heaven's Door go?

Paula (insistently): *Peter, darling, please let me in!*

St Peter: *You are a sinner, my child. A camel will sooner pass through the eye of a needle than you through this heavenly checkpoint.*

Paula (tearfully): *But haven't I atoned for my sins? I said sorry to that ugly old sister of mine even though she was the one who had committed adultery and – let's face it – fornicated like a mad rabbit behind her husband's back!*

St Peter (sternly): *You're doing it again! You're blaming your sister. You have to mean it. Say it like you mean it, for God's sake!*

Paula (genuinely): *I'm sorry. I truly am.*

'Don't worry. What's done is done,' I conceded defeat. In all honesty, I just wanted her out of my hair. I wondered if she had anywhere else to go: places to visit, people to haunt …

It appeared I was the only item on her agenda. She was on a mission to cleanse her soul and achieve redemption. She could not leave things unsaid. I was in for a long and torturous confession. She said, 'I was jealous. I wanted your life to myself. I thought it wasn't fair: you had it all, I had nothing.'

'You had an amazing career! Theatre, acting …'

'I was an understudy. In theatre and in life. You were the star. Still are. I envy you. I've always envied you. Even now.'

'Look at me, Paula! What's there to envy?'

She shrugged, unconvinced.

'All good things come to an end,' I commented philosophically, trying – in vain – to make her feel better. 'Look at me now – practically a vegetable!'

'A stubborn bloody turnip!' she chuckled.

'I think more of an aubergine,' I protested.

'Nope – a turnip! You've always been a turnip – the well-rooted, stubborn sort. I've no idea how you managed to get those men to love you, to *so* bloody love you.'

'What men?'

'Dad, for one –' Her crestfallen face looked endearing. I couldn't help but fall for it.

'You were the daddy's girl! He adored you!'

'Wrong!' She stomped her foot, like she used to when things didn't go her way. 'He merely looked after me, tried to keep me out of harm's way. But he *adored* you. He admired you, God knows for what … You mattered, only you. He didn't mind that much when I told him I was leaving. I was hoping he'd want to stop me, beg me to stay … I really needed him to say it: "*Stay, Paula, don't go*" … That's all he had to do. He would've done it for you. He would've begged you … But to me he said, "*It's your life, Paula. You wouldn't want me to tell you how to live it.*" I think he was relieved I was out of his hair.'

'You told him you were leaving?'

'I did. I told him and no one else. It was my call for help. But he didn't stop me. If he'd tried, things would've been … well, different, I suppose. I would've stayed; I would've married Rob. I knew him before you butted in –' Paula's accusatory glare went well with her running mascara and swollen eyelids. She was like an endangered species facing the final solution – a panda with a gun barrel stuck in its chest, looking the assassin in the eye.

'I had no idea you and Rob knew each other –'

'It's a small world.' The panda produced a resigned smile. Something dreamy and fuzzy spilled over her face. She couldn't help herself telling me every small detail – drill it into me. If it made her feel better, I was happy to take it in. 'It was a New Year's Eve street party, my first year in London. I clapped my eyes on Rob in Trafalgar Square. Masses of people, but he stood head and shoulders above the rest –'

'He's always been rather tall.' I don't know why I tried to sabotage her fairy tale. I guess I had every right to be slightly bitter. She gave me a supercilious glance and went on regardless.

'Everyone was drunk. Everyone was at it. Lights. Fireworks. He came from nowhere, a bit like Batman coming out of thick fog. Stood next to me. We danced. Well, we sort of danced – next to each other, you know, as if we weren't together but we only had eyes for each other. I said something. He said something. And I knew – he was my Mr Right.'

It all sounded very familiar. I was experiencing a strange sense of déjà vu. I was beginning to think my first encounter with Rob was a mere sequel to him and Paula, but I quickly convinced myself that it was theirs that amounted to nothing but a rehearsal.

Paula continued along the familiar path of a dark alleyway they had found in the backstreets of London where she mounted an empty beer crate –

'An empty beer crate so that I was high enough for him to enter me smoothly like a knife into butter,' I finished the sentence for her and she gaped at me, baffled.

'How did you know?'

'He did the same with me. Good old Rob,' I shrugged. 'He likes his routines.'

'It wasn't a routine!' Paula was typically quick to contradict me. 'It was spontaneous! It was real between us!'

'It always is the first time round,' I agreed. Who would have thought Rob had once been such a seasoned virginity snatcher? I should've guessed. Olivia was the living proof – she was bound to still be an unopened can, if slightly beyond the expiry date. Strangely, none of it seemed to matter to me any more. I was more concerned for Paula and her lofty delusions. I said, 'If I'd known you and … him. I wouldn't have dreamt of going between the two of you!'

Of course, I knew I would have. Rob had always been mine, but now, from the perspective of time, there was little purpose in making that point. I couldn't imagine my life without Rob and, conversely, I couldn't imagine Rob's life with Paula. It would've been a rollercoaster of emotional blackmail and a diet of seaweed and laxatives. I saved him but this point was rather academic at this stage of our earthly disintegration.

I promptly offered Paula my unequivocal apology. 'I'm sorry.'

Paula shook in frustration. 'Don't be daft! Stop apologising! You've always been so bloody stupid! Of course, Rob wouldn't have married me anyway. Our one-night stand didn't mean anything to him. Do you really think I have any doubts? If I had any, he had dispelled them on your wedding day.'

'Is that right? Is that what happened?' I was intrigued.

153

'I didn't know what to make of you two flirting –'

'*Us* two? I was flirting, he was avoiding me! He was so infuriatingly polite I almost puked! I gave him a choice. I opened my heart to him –' *Your legs, more likely*, I quipped inwardly, remembering her short red dress, '– but he said no. Plain and simple no. With the utmost courtesy, of course. He didn't want to upset me, but he loved you, you cow! I was nobody to him – well, just the bride's little sister. He'd love me like his own fucking sister. I was livid. Threw my Zippo at him.'

'Where was that?' At last, I was beginning to piece it all together.

'What does it matter – where? In the toilet, if you must know.'

'Men's toilet?'

'What if it was!'

'I saw you leaving the men's toilet. I thought you'd been getting off with someone. Such a romantic set-up …' My voice was teetering on the verge of breaking into a hearty chuckle.

'No, I was being rebuked by your groom. No pun intended, but he was on a high horse of marital fidelity, the fool! I threw my lighter at him. The mirror cracked. He picked up the lighter, handed it to me. His zip was still undone – I had caught him between the urinal and the washbasin in the loo, you see. I told him to stick it up his own arse. So there, so that you bloody well know: he loved you then and he still loves you now, the same way, and I don't think that will ever change.'

I could tell her about Olivia, but I didn't. Instead, I said: 'So what am I really: a turnip or a cow?'

'Both!' she blurted. Logic wasn't always her strongest quality, which was fortunate. I could go on humouring her. It was the least I could do for her – the woman had just killed herself! She needed some light relief.

She sat next to Tony, cocked her head, stretched her

long, scrawny neck, and peered into his eyes. 'What really got me was Tony,' she told me after a moment of watchful and serene adoration.

'Tony?'

'I could accept Rob. You and Rob – you're married for better or for worse, worse mainly, but married you are and I had to live with it. But when Tony told me about you and him ... that was the cherry on top.' She gave him a disdainful kiss. Oddly, he felt something, for he rubbed his left cheek as if he'd suffered a muscle spasm. Paula abandoned his side and glided towards me. I was still unnerved by her nakedness. Was she going to spend all eternity looking like that? It wasn't a savoury prospect. I could only hope that true to her nature, sooner or later, she would leave me behind and run away with some handsome bisexual angel. Meantime, she breathed into my ear, 'Tony was my idol. He was calm. Superior. He could deal with emotions. He was above all that daily pap of sentimentality. I worshipped him. And then he tells me about you. He drivels like a toothless dog ... You know what I thought? I thought: *Shit! The cow steals all my men! First Dad, then Rob. Now Tony.*'

'Don't tell me you also knew Tony first,' I teased, trying to avert my eyes from her.

'But I did!'

'You're joking?'

'I wish I was! We go back a long way, Tony and I. I know Tony like the back of my hand. At least, I thought I knew the bastard –'

'How on earth do you know Tony anyway?!'

Paula shrugged. 'There was this escort place – not a brothel! A respectable, high-class establishment frequented by influential people who needed intelligent company as much as they needed an occasional recreational fuck with no strings attached. You know the type: married to a boring old bag well past child-bearing age?'

I shook my head.

'Well, look in the mirror.' Paula was charmingly disarming. She really needn't wonder why she had no friends.

I wouldn't rise to her insults. 'So you had a career in prostitution?'

She winced at the word *prostitution*. 'I was sort of experimenting with sex, out of curiosity more than anything else. I was only eighteen – what did I know? I thought I could make a living out of selling my body. It was the only commodity I had after my own family had turned me out ...'

'Bollocks!' I had to protest. 'Your body is your own business, but what has all of that stuff to do with Tony?'

'I met Tony there.'

'In the brothel?' So Paula and Tony had met through the sex trade!

'Escort agency!'

'Of course! It's got a ring to it, doesn't it?' I quipped. 'We seem to sleep with the same men. Hey, as long as it stays in the family.'

'He wasn't a client, you daft girl! I didn't sleep with him. He was a boy for rent and I couldn't afford him. But I fell in love with him – we were so alike ... I told him, but I wasn't a viable proposition for him – we were friends, good friends, and he didn't want to soil what we had. He trusted me, and that alone was a huge compliment, coming from Tony! Tony doesn't trust anyone. I was the only one he trusted.' She thrust her Wimbledon-equipped chest forward and I nodded appreciatively, encouraging her to go on. She didn't need much encouragement.

'We used to talk a lot, Tony and I, the two musketeers!' I thought there were three of them, but didn't dare to point that out to my sister, who was galloping on her high horse into more revelations. 'We laughed at those old bastards with bloated guts and tiny dicks …' She paused for a smile at those comforting memories. 'When I came back to Bristol, I tracked him down. He was a big-shot lawyer by then, but he didn't change. Not really, not physically, not in any other way. He was still Tony – a lone wolf. I still loved him, and I told him so, again. That was when he told me about you! That was my cherry on top. It was bloody unbelievable! Was Rob not enough for you?!'

'It was just a meaningless fling,' I assured her.

'Not to Tony. He told me. He could still tell me a secret, and he did the very first day we met after so many years. He told me, and I remember his exact words. He said: *"You know, Paula, if I ever loved anyone, if I ever knew what it was to love someone, it is Georgie. It's her. How daft is that? The bloody stubborn, opinionated, tits out, bare-knuckles Georgie. No one has ever come close."* He told me that – in so many words.'

'You're such a fantasist, Paula! You'll never come down to earth! And let's face it, the chance of that happening now that you're –' I stopped halfway through the sentence. I shouldn't be antagonising poor Paula, but I charged on, on the defensive, in denial! I didn't want to hear it. Frankly, I just didn't want to be seduced by Tony all over again: I didn't want to believe he was capable of any feelings, especially for me. I had enough trouble fending off my feelings for him. It had taken considerable skill to convince myself about his callousness, for God's sake! It was so much easier to think him evil and the author of my misfortune. It was easier to shove him into the *I don't care* box. I didn't want to be obligated to care about him. There were enough people affected by my demise, people I should really worry about. Tony wasn't going to join that league – I couldn't allow that. I wouldn't allow that! I was hell-bent on weeding Tony out of my life… well, whatever was left of it.

'I've no reason to flatter you, believe me,' Paula

snorted. 'Anyway, he also mentioned that love was a highly overrated thing, hardly worth following through, if you must know the minute details.'

'That sounds more like the Tony I know. Still –'

Before I had a chance to further contemplate the meaning – and reliability – of Paula's revelation, Etienne emerged on the scene. He caught Tony's eye straight away, but Tony stayed put. He waited for the boy to come to him. Power games were his favourite pastime. He needed to stay in control, even if his trousers were bursting with a raging erection. Poor, delusional man!

The boy chatted to the barman; slowly his eyes travelled to Tony's table. He saw him despite the shadows, recognised him and stiffened. I don't believe it was the sexual kind of stiffening. The boy was afraid of Tony, not aroused by him. Nevertheless, he composed himself quickly and walked to Tony's table with a swagger.

'You need me?'

There was more than a sexual undertone to his question. Etienne was teasing Tony, establishing his new client's dependency on him.

'Sit down, Etienne,' Tony said calmly. There was a tiny glint of amusement in his eyes. Etienne saw it too, so he promptly dropped his seductive poise and slumped down in the chair next to Tony, the one only minutes ago vacated by the naked ghost of my sister.

'It's cold here,' he said.

'I do need you,' Tony ignored his observations about the room temperature. 'I need you to come to my house at six tonight, precisely at six.'

'I can't, not tonight. We can go now if you like. We don't have to be quick, but I will have to be gone by five. That gives us plenty of time, I'd think.'

'Six o'clock tonight, I said. There's a grand in it for you.'

158

Etienne's eyes lit up with greed. He was thinking, weighing up his options. 'It's a family occasion. A birthday – my gran's.'

'Gran will have to wait.'

'I'm happy to go with you now, but not later!' Etienne looked baffled. *What did it matter to the randy old fool if they got on with it now or at six in the evening? Was he going to get harder by six? Was the Viagra kicking in at six and not a minute earlier?* The boy's eyes narrowed. *Or was this some sort of premeditated group orgy? Gang rape of a young man by a bunch of twisted old bastards waving antique pistols in his face?*

'It's now or, I'm afraid, I'll have to give it a miss on this occasion.'

Tony smiled, 'Very businesslike. You'll go far, Etienne, but there won't be another occasion and I don't need you now. I need you at six p.m. tonight. There's a grand in it for you. No sex involved. Just an errand to run for me. You'll be back to your sweet old granny by eight. Take it or leave it.'

'What sort of errand?'

'You'll need to drive somewhere, and back.'

'That's all?'

'That's all.'

'Then why don't you ask someone else? A courier?'

'I trust you. I know enough about you to be able to trust you. Consider that a privilege. Or you can consider it a threat: I know enough about you to make your life hell, if you prefer it that way …'

'Just to drive somewhere?'

'I assume you can drive?'

'Of course I can.'

'So?'

Etienne's lips were dry. His juicy pink tongue ran over them like an artist's brush. 'I'll be there. A thousand pounds payable in advance?'

'Two hundred now, eight hundred on completion.'

Rob brought Olivia home! Like a pimply teenager with raging testosterone, he finally decided to turn his wet dreams into reality and get the girlfriend officially domiciled in his bedroom – *our* bedroom. Except that in their middle-aged world the starting point would be in the kitchen. And Olivia was there, to make the Sunday roast – on a Saturday! She had come equipped with orange Sainsbury's carrier bags bulging with goodness. Rob carried a few of them himself. They had gone shopping together! What could be more intimate than joint grocery shopping on Saturday morning? What could have more of the '*when two become one*'?

I shuddered. Even though, in my spiritually enhanced mind, I wished Rob every happiness in his new life *sans* me, I still couldn't find it within myself to rejoice. The kids shared my sentiment. They both looked mortified when, at the stroke of one, that cuddly blonde epitome of domesticity waddled into our kitchen laden with shopping bags.

'This is Olivia Pickles, my ... my work colleague,' Rob staggered through the preliminaries, sounding very unconvincing. Uncharitably, I contemplated the chances of Olivia being related to Eric Pickles. That gave me a modicum of consolation. 'She's offered – very kindly – to help with our dinner today.'

'I've heard of your dad's many cooking disasters in recent days,' she chirped in helpfully, clearly oblivious of the stir her entrance into our kitchen had created. 'I thought the least I could do was come to the rescue. If you don't mind?'

The cat, most certainly, didn't mind. As much as he was a timid creature and never came within stroking distance of me (my refusal to feed the creature may have had something to do with it), he immediately recognised

160

Olivia as a kindred spirit: an indulgent, cat-owning spinster. Intrigued by the smell of raw red meat in the house, he descended from his high pedestal in the lounge and entered the kitchen. He peered at her hopefully. Olivia had made an instant impression: with a purr of seductive foreplay, the feline began its rare ritual of rubbing himself against her legs.

Emma and Mark gaped wide-mouthed and speechless.

'It was a bit of a surprise for your dad, too!' She smiled and two enchanting dimples formed in her chubby cheeks. 'I called him to collect me from the shop. He thought he was just helping, you know, my car broke down or something. Imagine his surprise when I asked him to bring me here.'

'You're not the first one,' Mark mumbled under his breath. Rob shot him a warning glance, but it was too late.

'The other day we had this other "auntie" pop over, but she didn't look like she could cook. I'd say you're an improvement,' Emma added cruelly.

Paula shook with indignation. I found that vindicating, considering that only a few minutes earlier she had been gloating and basking in Rob's premature betrayal of the memory of me.

'Ah, your Auntie Paula!' Olivia was impervious to the insults. She was either too stupid to realise they were insults, or she didn't give a monkey's. Rob looked like he hoped it was the former.

'I'm useless at cooking. You remember that cheese on toast the other day, and the fireman?' he said to Emma.

'I remember your cheese on toast; I don't remember any firemen,' she replied sharply.

Olivia was unpacking the shopping: a blood-red joint of beef made it straight to the roasting pan which Rob had produced out of nowhere, astonishing me with his in-depth knowledge of our kitchen cupboard topography. The cat let out something closely resembling a yodel. While working salt and crushed garlic into the meat, Olivia said, 'I'm very sorry about your mum and I do hope she gets out of it unscathed, somehow ... I'm not trying to take her place – I wouldn't dream of that! I'm just trying to help your dad. Give you lot one square meal in a week. It must've been one hell of a week for all of you. Eating was, I'm sure, the last thing on your minds.'

'And the first thing on hers!' Paula commented. 'Who the hell is this woman?' she asked me. 'Do you know her? Did you know about her? Surely, you don't believe she's just a "*work colleague*"! Or is that what they call themselves these days?'

'Who?'

'Husband snatchers, who else! Watch out, that's exactly what she is!'

'And that's coming from you!' The meaningful elevation of my right eyebrow went unnoticed by my sister. 'Of course I know Olivia,' I lied. 'She works with Rob. It's true what he said.'

'You're either very stupid or very arrogant,' Paula retorted. 'They're having a *thing*. Are you blind?'

'That may explain why he rejected your blunt advances ...'

'You're such a bitch!' Paula hissed.

I was undeterred. 'Watch closely and learn. This is what men like – a bit of meat on the bone.'

Olivia was working her meat as if she were a masseur. She was rubbing oil into it, her fingers glistening as they slid up and down, and into every crevice. Rob watched, mesmerised. I dare not imagine what he was thinking those clever little chorizos could do to him.

Emma watched, too, her face twisted in horror. 'My stomach,' she said, grimacing, 'is still a bit tender. I don't think I can bear the sight of red meat.'

Olivia peered at Emma's skinny frame. She said nothing but her eyes said, 'Pity!'

Rob explained, 'Poor Emma, she threw up last night. All over ...'

'I'll go to my room,' Emma interrupted the delivery of further details.

Mark fidgeted uncomfortably. 'I'm not hungry either. I was thinking of visiting Mum.'

Visiting Chi, you mean, a nasty little voice whispered in my head. I suppressed it. Whatever their motivation, I was proud of my children. Their affections couldn't be bought cheaply: certainly not with a joint of meat and a few Brussels sprouts.

'Why don't we all go and visit Mum *after* dinner?'

Rob's mobile beeped. I was surprised he had it on. So was Paula. What happened to the texts she had sent to him – her cries for help? Why had he chosen to ignore them?

'What do you say? Should we eat first?' Rob continued, unfazed by the beep.

'Dad, it's your phone,' Emma said from the staircase. 'You've got a message.'

'Oh,' Rob fumbled through his deep pockets. He found the gadget, gazed at it mystified for a few seconds. 'I keep it on now that ... well, a phone call can come from the hospital any time ...' He coughed. 'Right, there! What do you know? There is a message. Two messages! How do I ... let me see ...' He must have pressed the right button. 'God,' his head shook as he inhaled sharply. 'It's from Paula. I must go. Sorry, it may be nothing, but –'

At last! I was rid of Paula. She accompanied Rob to her flat to witness the discovery of her body and take careful notes of his reactions. Deep down, she believed there was a sliver of hope that she could be revived. I knew otherwise, but she still had to find out for herself. At least there would now be the spectacle of shock, of grief, friends and enemies remembering this bright but short-lived star – all the things and theatrics Paula held dear. I thought the least I could do was to afford her some privacy in this trying moment. I followed my son to my hospital bedside.

Indeed, he made it as far as my room, but he wasn't really there to hold my limp hand. His head swivelled round and round as he searched for Chi. Every time steps resonated on the linoleum of the long, brightly lit corridor, he was up from the chair, poking his head out, looking for her.

The hospital was busy, as you would expect it to be at the weekend: grapes-and-biscuits-laden visitors threaded uncertain navigation routes amongst hospital wards, looking lost and frightened, peering into rooms, checking bed occupants, sighing with silent relief to find their loved ones still in one piece and holding on to life. Others weren't so lucky … Next door to me, a woman shrilled. It was either a rat or someone had died. I thought I should check. In a six-bed room, the middle bed on the right was empty. The shrilling woman had thrown herself across it, cuddling a crumpled pillow, whilst other patients watched in silence.

'Oh God … he's gone …' She lifted her head from the pillow and gazed around the room, looking for an explanation. 'When did it happen? The hospital never called –'

A skinny man with deep-set eyes and sunken cheeks spoke from the bed by the window: 'They've taken Ross for a scan. Keep your voice down, madam, I'm trying to read.' And he picked up a newspaper – the *Guardian*, I noted; a level-headed and sensible man, then, whose word could be relied upon.

The woman peeled herself off the bed and stormed out of the room, calling for the nurse. 'Why are we not informed? There aren't any communication channels –'

I heard her shrilling some more, but this time in the

nurses' station. In the relative sanctity of my room, Mark patted my hand and said, 'Mum, have you seen that Vietnamese nurse today at all? Her name is Chi.' It was nice of him to share, I thought, it was a sign of growing trust between us.

'I'd better tell you before you find out from someone else: I'm in love with her. I don't know if you ever felt that way …' It was a good question, I had to give it to him. *Had I ever felt that way? Had I ever been in love? Can you be in love and in control at the same time? Because if you can't, then, well … I had never lost control. I had always known when to pull back or when to push on. But,* I thought, *I cared. I cared, and that would have to do for now.*

'It's an odd feeling. It won't let you sleep at night because you're anxious not to lose them. You know? Like when you wake up in the morning, will they still be there? I'm shit-scared of losing her. She's so tiny and so elusive. I suppose you'd say all Vietnamese are tiny and elusive, but she's the only Vietnamese person I know. The only one I love. I must take care of her. I wish you were conscious at least, so I could introduce her to you.' He kept patting my hand mechanically as he was breaking out his news to me, and breaking out in a cold sweat as well. 'But you know her already. You do! She's that little nurse that comes here every day to check on you. Yep, that's her: the love of my life. Chi – it means a twig in Vietnamese –'

'Bastard!'

It was unmistakably Charlotte's voice. I had missed her arrival as much as Mark had. She had crept up on us both. There she stood with her blonde locks foaming around her face, her cheeks flushed with fury – a scorned Nordic Valkyrja.

'Charlotte?' Mark was taken aback. He got up from the chair, knocked it down. It clunked. Instinctively, he looked

165

at me to check if that woke me up. I wished!

'How could you? We've only just –' She glanced at her engagement finger, unsure if what she believed was her engagement ring was really there.

'I'm sorry, Charlotte ... You and I – we didn't really think it through ... I was going to ...'

'What were you going to do? What?' Her fury was transforming into hysteria. 'You bloody bastard! What are you trying to do to me? Kill me?'

'I'd never ... Never would I want to hurt you. The last person on this planet, I'd want to hurt, believe me, is you. But it happened –'

'You're taking the piss? Why are you doing this to me?'

'I'll explain, calmly. Give me a chance. Let's not do it here, by my mother's bedside.'

'Let's not!' She was pulling at her finger as if her objective was to tear it away from her hand.

Down the corridor Chi was approaching, dressed in her nurse's uniform. She was heading for my room. I could tell she was alarmed. The argument could be heard from afar; the whole hospital floor was tuning in.

Finally, Charlotte managed to pull the engagement ring off her finger, without taking her finger with it. She waved the ring in Mark's face. 'What is this? A joke? Is this your engagement ring or not? You gave it to me, remember?'

'I ... I ... You can keep it. Please keep it, but –'

Outpouring of tears prevented her from speaking. She threw the ring at him. It ricocheted from his shoulder and landed on my bed. She burst out, retching with tears. For a split second, Mark just stood there, shocked. Her steps and sobs were receding down the corridor. 'Shit!' he mumbled, and took off, after her. In the corridor he brushed by Chi. At first, he didn't recognise her, then he stopped a few steps past her. Looked back. Hesitated. Gave her an apologetic, plaintive gaze, and ran after Charlotte.

Chi lowered her eyes and bit her bottom lip, turned and walked slowly, placing her feet firmly: one in front of the other. She passed by a few nurses and visitors, all staring curiously at her and then retreating back into their chores and conversations with their loved ones.

She sought refuge from the public eye in my room. She knew I wouldn't judge her. And I wouldn't. Somehow, despite myself and against common sense, I was on her side. I thought Mark was a fool. A week ago I would have rejoiced, but today I felt he was the loser, not Chi.

Her hands were trembling ever so slightly when she checked the valves on my life support machine and recorded data on my patient board. As she was straightening my sheets and smoothing out the blanket, she found the ring. She picked it up, turned it in her fingers and watched it sparkle against the lights. Then she put it on my bedside table. Her face showed no emotion, but her cheeks were wet.

Charlotte thundered down the fire escape. Mark was only a few steps behind her, but she was a fast runner. She wasn't an athlete for nothing. She crossed the foyer, pushing forward blindly. Instinctively, people made way for her: she had that haunted look of someone who had been told their loved one was dead and that there was nothing that could be done to bring them back.

Walking in long strides, but refusing to run (not to make a spectacle of himself – a genetic trace of the Ibsens he had inherited), Mark stood little chance of catching up with her. As she charged across the forecourt, thrusting herself at oncoming traffic, he seemed to be slowing down in his pursuit of her. It was now more out of concern for her safety than for the purpose of catching up with her that he was following her at all. He gestured to the driver of an approaching four-by-four to stop and give way. When the man did so, Mark paused by his window and wheezed breathlessly, 'Thanks! She's distraught.'

'Yeah, no problem!' the driver responded. ''Tis an 'ospital, innit? Things 'appen!'

'Thanks!'

He chased her across the vast hospital parking area, all the way to her car. It was a small, battered Ford, grey and unassuming, totally out of sync with its glamorous owner. From a distance of several metres, Charlotte pressed the immobiliser's button. The car winked at her cheerfully. She was almost in when Mark abandoned his pursuit, stood dead in his tracks and shouted, 'Charlotte!'

A row of cars separated them. As she turned to face him, they could only see each other from the chest up. A glimmer of hope lit in her eyes. 'Yes, Mark?' The same, faint hope rang in her voice.

He put his arms up in the air. 'I am sorry it's come to this,' he told her. 'I am sorry you had to find out that way … But I can't keep lying to you. Sorry …'

The glimmer of hope exploded into a firework of fury. 'Bastard!'

'Please take care –'

'Fuck off.' She slammed the door, thrust the beam of headlights into his face, and drove off with an ominous screech of tyres.

Chi was still by my bedside, taking time to compose herself before she emerged to face the world at large and pretend convincingly that what had just happened was all water off a duck's back. Without much purpose, she was re-arranging my pillows for the umpteenth time. Mark caught her unawares when he spoke, still panting, 'Did you really think I was going to let you go?'

She spun on her heel.

'I told you, Chi – you are *it* for me! I bloody well love you and won't ever lose you!'

He ran to her and lifted her – her feet dangling above

the floor – and squeezed her so hard that she squealed. 'Put me down! Put me down before someone sees you and they throw us out of here! Put me down, you madman!' she chimed with laughter.

'Not before you say you'll marry me!'

Personally, I thought he was overdoing it. His first bride wasn't yet cold in her grave – so to speak – and here he was proposing to the next one. Great minds think alike and I had proof of it when Chi pointed to Charlotte's ring glittering furiously on my bedside table. 'Do you not think you should take a break from marriage for a day or two?' she asked.

'I haven't started yet. Not with the right woman!' Mark insisted, still holding her up in the air like a squirming beetle. 'Say yes, please,' he said. 'I won't rest till you do.'

'On one condition.'

'Name it.'

'You won't force me to stay here. And you won't give me a recycled ring.'

'That's two conditions. Both accepted.' Mark put her down, fell to one knee, grabbed her hand and kissed it. Then, still on his knee, he spoke to me: 'Mum, meet Chi – my wife to be.'

I must admit, I was bruised and swollen with emotions. Perhaps for the first time I was glad my horrid misadventure had befallen me. At least I didn't have to struggle to hold back tears of joy and stop myself from jumping through the roof – I was gracefully bedridden and unable to raise a finger.

Etienne was punctual. He rang the doorbell at precisely six o'clock. Tony opened the door almost instantly, as if he was standing behind it, waiting. He was dressed oddly for the occasion of his date: dark-grey joggers, brand new and untypically cheap trainers with no labels, dark-green khaki coat and a beanie that made his head appear pear-shaped.

Etienne ran his eyes up and down his benefactor's strange attire without comment.

'Step in,' Tony led him to the kitchen. 'Sit down.'

Etienne looked around him nervously. He relaxed a bit once he had established that there was no one in the house but the two of them and that neither the bedroom nor a mysterious cellar behind a concealed trapdoor was on the cards. 'So, you want me to drive somewhere?'

There was a map of Bristol on the kitchen table. It was opened on a page that depicted the convoluted arteries of the eastern suburbs. Tony stabbed his fingers at a spot marked in pencil. 'I want you to go there. It's where the old Cadbury factory used to be.'

'Yes, I know that area. Why?'

'No reason.'

Etienne fidgeted uncomfortably. I would be bloody nervous too if I were him.

'I need to know,' he said. 'I need to know what's there and why I'm wanted there. Otherwise I won't do it. There's a limit to what I'm prepared to do – even for a thousand pounds.'

'You're not needed there. Neither are you *wanted* there. What I want you to do is to get there via this route,' Tony ran his finger along what looked like a stretch of ring road. He paused at a spot, 'Somewhere here you'll see a speed camera. It's active. I want you to go over the limit: ten or fifteen miles over, no more.'

'I'll get caught.'

'You'll get a picture taken. Driving my car. *I* will get caught,' Tony corrected him. 'Be there around 7 p.m., give or take twenty minutes, understood?'

'You want to get speeding points? You're bonkers?' Etienne stared at him, incredulous. 'I don't believe you. What's going on? What are you getting me into?'

Tony exhaled slowly. 'Nothing to worry about. I want to establish a false alibi. I need to be somewhere else without anyone knowing. You'll get me caught on the camera at the right time in a different place. Does that make sense?'

'Why do you need to be –'

'You'd be better off not knowing. Do we have a deal?'

Etienne nodded.

'OK. After speeding by the camera, you will go all the way to that factory. Drive around it. Stop somewhere at the back of it for about quarter of an hour. Have a smoke, or something – look out of place. Someone might see you, CCTV cameras may register you if they're working. Wear this jacket, hood up.' He passed him a nondescript waterproof, which was bound to make the boy look bulkier than he was in reality. 'Discreetly, from inside the car, take a photo of the loading zone at 7.30 on this camera.'

'Why?'

'For my peace of mind. I want to be sure you got there. Not that I don't trust you.'

Etienne smiled.

'Drive back here down the same route. Don't speed on your way back. Be here by eight.' Tony threw a key to his young accomplice. I couldn't believe he would entrust his magnificent MGA into the hands of a casual male escort. But he did. Something greater was at stake here, and I dreaded to think what it was.

As soon as Etienne was out of the door, Tony went to his weapon display cabinet. Before handling the guns, he put on black leather gloves. I knew which pistol he would go for: the untraceable one. He took it out, checked that it was loaded, wrapped it in a cloth, and placed it gently into a rucksack, which he slung over his shoulder. Thus armed, he went to the kitchen where, in a bottom drawer full of every man's useful objects, he collected what looked like a car key. He headed for the garage. Unbeknown to me (and I imagine unbeknown to the world at large), the garage housed an old and inconspicuous Ford Fiesta, at least ten years old if the square bodywork was anything to go by. Tony got in. The engine started straight away.

It was twenty past six when Tony drove away in the navy blue Fiesta, carrying an unlicensed pistol and heading for Clifton. My blood ran cold. You didn't have to be a genius to work out what he was up to. Tony didn't trust anyone, only himself. He was a suspicious beast: a perfectionist. In all the cases he handled there were never loose ends left dangling for his opponents to pull and unravel. It was Tony who ran the show, Tony who controlled every minute aspect. He didn't trust his juniors, or even his partners to put his cases together for him. He did it himself. He most certainly didn't trust Ehler to 'sort out' Jason Mahon. Tony was going to do the sorting out himself. Too much was at stake for him: if Jason was finally apprehended, he would lead the police to Ehler, and then to Tony. They had already made the connection; all they needed now were witnesses. Tony was planning to get rid of them, at least one of them, the weakest link: Jason Mahon. He probably guessed Ehler would try to silence the boy by paying him off or bullying him into submission, but Jason had already proved himself unreliable in this department. He had been prepared to testify against his master once before, what could stop him now? Tony wouldn't take the chance of finding out. The boy had to be silenced permanently and irreversibly. Hence the pistol. I had no doubt Tony would use it. I didn't want him to do it – this whole affair was getting out of hand – but Tony didn't need my permission. He wasn't doing it for me. He was doing it to save his skin, and in that mission he would stop at nothing. Etienne would provide him with a cast iron alibi. Ehler would keep his mouth shut and would get rid of the boy's body quickly and efficiently. He would have nothing on Tony without implicating himself, so if he suspected anything he would keep it to himself. After all, he was in it up to his eyeballs. If the body was ever found, the trail would lead to Ehler – and it would stop there. Tony would walk away squeaky clean.

I watched with dread as the Fiesta zoomed down Upper Belgrave Road, heading for Clifton Down. Suddenly it stopped. There was a parking space on the side of the road by Bristol Zoo. Tony indicated and reversed into the space. I was baffled: was he, after all, planning a quiet evening at the zoo, at his worst perhaps venturing into shooting a couple of annoying penguins or a cheeky monkey?

My hope was short-lived. Tony walked off in the opposite direction, towards the street where Michael Ehler lived. Of course, it would be unwise to park right in front of Ehler's mansion. Tony had really thought it through. He parked where masses of anonymous people were parking all day long, where endless numbers of mums, kids and grannies passed by, paying not the slightest attention to one mediocre old Ford Fiesta.

It was a long walk from the zoo to Ehler's house, and it was already quarter to seven. Tony broke into a gentle jog. There were many joggers out on the College Fields – nothing unusual about one with a rucksack on his back. I crossed my virtual fingers and wished to God that Tony would be run over by a car or that he tripped and sprained his ankle, but he proceeded undisturbed to his final destination.

At five minutes past seven Tony sneaked up the steep pathway leading to Ehler's garden and positioned himself only metres away from the large patio door of Ehler's study. He was well concealed amongst the wild shrubbery that brimmed over every inch of the garden. He unzipped the pocket of his rucksack where he had earlier deposited the gun.

The whole house was shrouded in darkness, at first sight

uninhabited. Only the study was brightly lit. Jason was there already. He was very animated: his arms had a life of their own. He was pacing, stopping suddenly, turning, and fidgeting. His nerves had to be a bundle of live wires. Not an easy target, but I guess Tony was used to all sorts of moving targets that needed pacifying.

I admired his composure. True to form, he watched the scene before him with a steady gaze. His hands, folded peacefully on the gun as if it was a Sunday Missal, were perfectly still.

Ehler was sitting in a high-backed chair behind a desk, looking like a mythical Godfather. At one point, he got up and gestured to the agitated Mahon to shut up. Mahon froze, then smiled. It looked like he was thanking Ehler: he was nodding submissively; his hands were pressed together as if in prayer. Ehler put his hand on the young scoundrel's back; patted him in an indulgent, paterfamilias manner. They both laughed.

Tony removed the gun from the cloth. Cocked it. Pointed it at the two people in the study.

Ehler moved away, leaving Jason exposed. I forgave the little weasel long ago. I didn't want him dead. I didn't want Tony to kill him. For grief's sake, he was only a pimply teenager! It would be such a pointless death! If only I could press the stop button on a remote control and bring it all to a halt …

Tony was watching as Ehler opened a safe in the wall behind a section of books which were obviously only painted on the safe's door. Money! He was probably giving Jason money to get out of the country – something like that. I was OK with that. Why couldn't Tony be?

He pointed the gun.

Instead of a nice little parcel of banknotes, Ehler pulled out a pistol and aimed it at Jason. Jason fell to his knees, holding his face in his hands. Tony remained unperturbed. Only now did I notice he wasn't pointing his weapon at

Jason, but at Ehler. Before the fat man pulled the trigger, Tony shot him. He then promptly wrapped the cloth around the gun and returned it to his rucksack. He clearly had no intention of shooting Jason as well. In a matter of seconds he was out of the garden, jogging lightly down the stone steps and weaving into the evening's steady flow of foot traffic.

I had to be out of there, too. In the back of my mind, etched there for ever, was the massive body of Michael Ehler lying flat on its back, the big gut spilled like a melting ice-cream, hands outstretched, eyes staring into the wood-panelled ceiling of his study. There was a neat hole in his forehead: the entry point of the bullet. Tony had shot him in the head. It was a precision shot – an assassin's job. I didn't want to look back, see what Mahon would do. He was probably in shock. The whole house was on alert. Someone had called the police. Game over.

I went home.

I didn't expect Olivia to be there. Neither did I expect her and Rob to be sitting at my kitchen table, over roast dinner and a glass of red wine. For some strange reason I had thought that the world had momentarily come to a standstill as murder reigned supreme at the other end of town. No such thing – life has this habit of going on, regardless. People eat dinner and drink wine while other people are busy blowing each others' brains out.

The beef was well overcooked, but then it was originally meant to be eaten sometime around 3 p.m., at the approximate time of Rob's unscheduled visit to Paula's.

'It was a terrible sight,' Rob was telling Olivia, who was squashing a Brussels sprout into thick gravy. 'Like she was having a bath in her own blood. The water was cold – she must've done it in the morning, just as she sent me the text.'

175

'You checked the water? Did you put your hand in it?' Olivia grimaced. She had a green sprout leaf on a front tooth.

'I tried to pull her out. Don't know what I was thinking ... First instinct, I suppose ... But she was well gone: cold, stiff as a ...' Rob's dinner stood untouched. At least he had the decency not to be able to swallow. 'I called an ambulance, though I knew she was gone.'

Paula glanced at me and said: 'They didn't bother checking my pulse or perform any ... what you call it? CRP? They just said "rigor mortis". Can you believe that? I could wake up in one of those dreadful fridges in a mortuary and die of fright because nobody bothered to check my pulse!'

'You can't die again, Paula – you're already dead,' I reminded her, and shuddered. She was still stark-naked and dripping wet. 'Can you not put something on, for God's sake!'

'I can't do anything about my looks post-mortem any more than you can,' she retorted. 'Do you realise you've been floating about with bloody snot hanging out of your nose all this time? Except I'm too polite to point it out to you.'

'You just did.'

'They took her away in a body bag. It was awful,' Rob went on as Olivia put a piece of beef in her mouth and started chewing it thoughtfully. 'Then I had to wait for the police. It was a suicide – unnatural death, you see, they had to interview me, the usual ...' Rob winced. 'Except, nothing is usual any more, is it? Georgie in a coma, Paula slashing her wrists, and my daughter involved with some fireman who could be mixed up in Georgie's accident ... Sometimes I'm sure – damn sure – this is one of those dreams that doesn't make any sense, but feels too real for comfort, and that I'll wake up any minute to see Georgie walk through that door after her evening run, and on

Monday I'll go to work as I do every Monday, and see you, and feel better for it –'

Olivia put her hand on his to stop it from juddering. She said, 'I'm here already.'

Paula raised an eyebrow. 'And so life goes on, and you're not even dead yet.'

'But the man who got that juvenile dickhead to run me over, is,' I told her. 'Tony's just shot him in the head.' It was at this point, as I got it off my chest, that I fell apart. I cried, and cried like a baby, and my egotistical sister had no idea how to stop me.

Olivia and Rob were onto the pudding (gelatinous trifle with fresh raspberries) when I finished telling Paula what I had just witnessed at Ehler's house.

'He did it for you!' she exclaimed, a spark of jealousy in her panda's eyes. 'Poor Tony! You don't realise how much he loves you, you silly cow! He punished that man for hurting you … He is your knight in shining armour, your lord protector, your lover, your man! How romantic!'

'You are an idiot, Paula,' I commented coldly. Yes, perhaps Tony did do it for me, a misguided attempt at putting things right, atoning for his betrayal, but even if that, and not his own skin, was his motivation, I wouldn't be seen, dead or alive, condoning it. It was wrong and I, of all people, should know that. I'd get people locked up for life for things like that. The bestiality of it all, the raw callousness … And yet, deep down, I was turned on. He would never let me go! He had me in the palm of his hand and no matter how hard I kicked and how loud I screamed in denial, I couldn't get him out of my mind. Not to mention my guilt. It was my fault! I told him too much. I blabbered and boasted that I would have his client's balls on the golden platter. I toyed with his ego, challenged him and released the beast from within him. I played with fire and I got burned. Tony only struck a match. Now the wildfire was spreading and we were both trapped in it.

Not surprisingly, the children weren't sharing in the family meal. Mark was still in hospital, by my side, or rather following Chi on her rounds, like a pubescent puppy. Emma was in her room upstairs, 'down with an upset tummy', or rather dwelling on her lost innocence and hatred of men. She was lying on her bed, staring at the bare walls dotted with greasy smudges of Blu-Tac that used to hold her gothic posters in place. Though she wasn't crying, her eyes were red and swollen and her cheeks were patchy with colour. If I could come back to life just for a bit, it would be to hold my child, kiss her patchy cheeks and tell her that this wasn't that bad at all, that there would be dozens of boyfriends, some of whom would betray her, some of whom she would betray, but it wasn't the end of the world – it was just how life went. Being hurt was part of being alive, and it would pass.

Her telephone rang. She checked the screen and saw Brandon's name. Her face flushed red. She hesitated and wondered what to do until the call went to the voicemail. 'Bastard,' she reminded herself, but despite that reminder, called her mailbox to listen to his voice. Except that he had left no message. She looked even more hurt. Suddenly her mobile rang again. She answered immediately.

'Emma, I just came back from the police station. They kept me almost all day, asking millions of questions –'

'Yes, it was me. I told them about you and Jason. Is that it? Is that what you wanted to know? Who snitched on you?'

'I'm not trying to blame you, I understand.'

'I don't need your understanding. Or your forgiveness,' she sniffled.

'I would've done the same.'

'Good. I must go.'

'Please don't go!' Panic stole into his voice.

I could see from her face that she wouldn't be able to

178

put the phone down on him. 'What do you want, Brandon? We're over.'

'I want to explain. I knew nothing about your mother! I had nothing to do with what happened to her!'

'You knew Jason ran her over in a stolen car. I heard you two arguing that day when I stopped by at yours. Don't lie to me. Don't fall even lower than you already are.'

'Yes, yes, I knew he did something stupid, but I didn't know he was going to do it, if you know what I mean? I didn't put him up to it. Do you understand?'

'No. I don't want to listen to you any more.'

'After the fact, after he'd done it, he told me he knocked over some woman in the street, that his boss told him to do it to scare her off, or something ... He regretted it. He was shit-scared, but he couldn't take it back, could he? What was I supposed to do?'

'Telling the police would be an option,' she said coldly.

'I told the cops. I told them all I knew!'

'Only after I shopped you!'

There was a long pause. His breathing was frantic on the other side of the phone. He was thinking hard, thinking fast – he had no defences left. Yet he didn't want to lose her. 'Emma, I didn't know how bad it was ... Jason was a friend ... he trusted me ... He looked up to me ... I couldn't ... There are limits ... And I didn't know it was your mother! If I knew, believe me –'

'Whoever it was, it just isn't right! It wasn't right for you to cover up for him. Whoever she was, she was somebody's mum, or daughter, or just *someone*!' Emma might only have been approaching sixteen but she had the moral compass of an adult. I was proud of her.

'Yes ... you're right. I don't want to argue. I've no right to argue with you over this.' He sighed. 'I love you. Can you try to forgive me? I'll do anything.'

'I can't ...'

179

There was a thunderous, impatient knock on Brandon's door. I heard him shout, 'Go away! Not now! Fuck off!' Then he spoke into the telephone, 'Emma, you can … Please …'

Before Emma answered, a sudden commotion and the shattering sound of a door being broken in had stopped her in her tracks. She listened. There were voices – Brandon's: shouting, telling someone to fuck off and somebody else's voice pleading for help. Both voices were indistinct, coming from a distance. It seemed Brandon had dropped his mobile without hanging up.

Emma sat up on her bed and pressed the telephone hard against her ear. I was curious about what was going on at Brandon's, but I couldn't bring myself to leave her. Though she wasn't there with him, though she wasn't in direct danger, I felt absolutely compelled to stay with her and look after her. Brandon, on the other hand, was a big boy – he could look after himself.

Within seconds we both knew that the intruder was Jason. He was still in shock, blathering uncontrollably, whispering, shouting and sobbing – all in equal measure: 'Brandon, mate, you got to help me! Boss shot himself. In front of me. Fuck, fuck, fuck!'

'You're fucking bleeding, Jason. I'll call an ambulance.'

'No, no fucking ambulance. It's his blood. It's gone all over me. Look, fuck me!' Obviously Jason had only just realised he was covered in Ehler's blood. He was probably looking at himself in the mirror, losing his mind all over again, trying to make sense of events and bring some order to his head.

'I thought he was gonna shoot me … No, first, first he was givin' me cash to get out of town, then he points a gun at me, then he puts a bullet in his own head. Like – fuck me! Like he don't know what he's doing. Right in the middle, here!'

I was beginning to put two and two together: Jason had covered his eyes before Ehler pulled the trigger. He had seen nothing. He'd only heard the shot and then saw Ehler's body sprawled before him with a bullet through his head. The first thought that occurred to the poor little weasel was: Boss shot himself! I can't imagine how he had justified this sudden change of heart to himself – perhaps Boss had experienced a pang of conscience and turned against himself to atone for all his sins and trespasses?

'Jason, I'm calling the cops. You can tell them everything.' I wondered if Brandon was saying that for Emma's benefit, but it was the first sensible thing he had said all evening.

'No fucking way!' Jason disagreed. 'They'll pin it on me. They'll do me in for that woman anyhow. I ain't goin' down.'

'That woman is Emma's mother!'

Silence. Were they whispering to each other? Was there a sudden explosion of sign language in that room – the boys rehearsing a joint version of events? Then Jason screeched, 'I didn't know, did I! I didn't, I swear!'

'I'm calling the cops.'

'You! You'll fucking go down with me, try me!' Menace stole into Jason's voice. He was desperate.

'What have I done, Jason?'

'You told me, you bastard! You said, "follow your dreams! Go and get it, Jason! Grab life by the feet!" I learned your shit by heart. I lived by it!'

'I didn't fucking tell you to kill anyone!'

'One and the same thing!'

'No! No, Jason! No, it isn't. You're such an *arse*! I'm calling the cops.'

'Look here! Look, I got money …' The despair distorted Jason's voice turning it into a teenage boy's high-octave shrill. 'Ehler's safe was full of it. Millions! Look here! Yeah, half is yours. Yeah? Just help me, you fuck!'

'I don't want to have anything to do with it. I'm calling the cops,' Brandon's voice was now very close to the phone. He must have picked it up to dial 999.

Jason howled. It wasn't any coherent statement, just a strangled war cry. A scuffle followed. Someone croaked. Something fell to the floor with a clank. A thud. A 'Sorry, sorry mate!' was whispered with dread, followed by a muffled cry. The slamming of a door. Receding steps.

Emma screamed into her telephone: 'Brandon? Brandon! Speak to me!'

Nothing.

Then a faint wheeze.

'Em, I've been stabbed. I'm bleeding ...'

Rob, Olivia, Paula, and I crowded over Emma. She was calm and collected, almost as if this whole affair had nothing to do with her. 'I want to report a stabbing – 18 Gaolers Road – that's g-a-o-l-e-r-s. Correct,' she nodded, unnecessarily, to the emergency services operator who was on the other end of the line. 'No, it isn't me. The ... victim is bleeding – you must send an ambulance immediately. And a police car. Inform Inspector Thackeray. The attacker, Jason Mahon, is already wanted by the police. May still be there. I think he's armed. No, I'm not there. Brandon – the victim – called me on the phone. *My* name? Emma Ibsen. Can we leave details until later? Get the paramedics there, now.' I was mightily impressed with her composure.

Rob, Olivia, and Paula were mystified. Paula looked at me strangely, 'Is this a prank call?'

'No,' I replied curtly. I had no time for lengthy clarifications. In any event I wasn't sure what had really happened.

Only when Emma put the phone down could we all see she was shaking like a leaf. Her nerves were shot. 'Dad?' She gazed at Rob with horror in her eyes. 'If Brandon dies, it'll be my fault. I drove him to it. I drove him to take Jason on. And now he's bleeding to death.'

'Well, surely it can't be that serious!' Rob found it hard to believe that someone as young as Emma could be mixed up with something as grim as 'bleeding to death'. 'Boys will be boys … a little scuffle … Is that what it was?'

Olivia put a maternal arm around Emma's shoulders. 'You've done the right thing. One can't be too careful. Now, let's go to the kitchen. I'll make you a cup of tea.'

'Is she for real?' Paula stared. 'The girl needs a shot of brandy, not a sodding cup of tea!'

Luckily Emma couldn't hear either of them. She gazed at Rob pleadingly. 'I need to be at the hospital when they bring him there. I'll never forgive myself if he dies. Please, Dad, can we go? Can we go now?'

Of course, it wasn't Emma's fault – silly child! Somewhere in the deepest recesses of my subconscious mind I knew the fault was mine. I had attracted death and destruction to my family. It was as if my accident created a domino effect where one piece after another – one life after another – got knocked down in a chain reaction of self-perpetuating revenge. I seemed to have been holding on to life like a drunk falling down from his seat at the head of a dining table and pulling with him the table cloth and all that was on it. It had to stop! They all had to break away from me: Tony, Jason, Brandon, Emma, Rob, Mark … I had to break away from them before I took them all with me.

The call came to Rob's mobile as they sat waiting outside the operating theatre. Brandon had been taken for surgery. He had been stabbed in the abdomen, but that was all the doctors could say. No one knew if any vital organs had been damaged. In the silence of an empty hospital corridor where only a few departing souls rattled about, the ringing of Rob's mobile phone sounded like a church bell summoning mourners to a funeral service.

'Dad,' Mark sounded hollow. 'It's Mum. She's dying.'

Wow! That came as a surprise. I admit I had been contemplating the possibility of that happening – everybody had – but death takes us by surprise even when we expect it. It is the feeling of being robbed in broad daylight. Our righteous indignation prevents us from accepting it, despite knowing that it's coming and there is no stopping it. It's the violation of us, the violation of our existence, the kind of crime where we, the victims, receive the sentence. Death sentence. It takes us to the one place where we can't plead innocence, because our innocence doesn't matter.

And yet, despite my indignation, I considered myself very lucky indeed. I wasn't dying alone. What was the chance of everyone I loved being there, by my deathbed, right on cue! They ran across the hospital wards, corridors and stairs, and within minutes they were with me. Chi was applying compressions to my chest, her small body pulsating like a pneumatic pump. The little screen on my life support machine was showing a pair of bright, flat lines. *Someone kick that computer!* I screamed, *it's broken!* No one listened. They joined Mark in the helpless admiration of Chi's efforts.

Within seconds Dr Jarzecki arrived on the scene with two other nurses pulling in an arsenal of death-defeating weaponry. The good doctor glanced at the lined screen and shook his head, but nevertheless he decided to give me a go. A pair of what I'd describe as jump-leads was thrust at my chest – my body jerked and convulsed. Then it fell back, limp and unresponsive. Another go – another chance. And I missed it again.

Dr Jarzecki screamed at the nurses. 'Adrenalin, sister! Now! She is SLEEPing away!'

Rob stared at him, confused. 'She's sleeping?' he asked, cautiously hopeful.

'No, *slipping* away,' Mark translated the good doctor's vernacular into standard English. 'She's slipping away.'

No one had anything to add. Silence becomes death, I thought. Their silence was almost soothing; it was restorative, like catching breath between high notes.

Until Mother spoke.

'Bound to catch you two jumping the queue! Ever heard of waiting for your parents to die first? It's only common courtesy, but *nooo*, not the two of you! You've always been so competitive! Always me, me, me ... Always me first!'

There she was, our good old supercilious mother, less the stale biscuit and cold tea, less the twisted stockings, less the grey hair and convoluted spine bent by osteoporosis. She was back to her forties – her power years, wearing the bell-bottom trousers and the psychedelically patterned blouse I remembered her wearing when Paula and I had been little girls.

'I am *not* burying the two of you, forget it! Anyway, as things are I wouldn't have anything to wear for two funerals. I couldn't wear the same outfit – what would people say? We'll just have to die together, on three, holding hands. One, two, three –'

We used to do things together, *on three*. When we were afraid of something – like going to a dentist for a check-up or running into the sea when the waves were high – Mother would make us hold hands – all three of us – and she would say: one, two, three – and we would say 'JUMP!' It used to make things easy.

'Mummy? Is that you?' Both Paula and I spoke simultaneously – on three, as it were. Funny how after all those years of distance and formality, we instantly reverted to calling her *Mummy*, just as we had when we were little.

'That's me. Stroke, heart attack, dying peacefully in my sleep – choose one,' she said, rather cheerfully considering the circumstances under which we found ourselves reunited. 'Fact is, I didn't create much fuss with my passing. You, on the other hand,' she pointed an accusatory finger at Paula, 'did push the boundary a fraction too far – your own fault, no one else's!'

'Oh, Mum, do you have to? Don't you think I know it?'

'A bit too late knowing it now! Typical Paula: act first, think later … and as for you,' she glared at me, 'you've always been too arrogant for your own good. Someday, someone was bound to put you in your place. And, for God's sake,' she passed me a handkerchief, 'wipe that snot off your face!'

Our darling mother was on form: unfair, as usual. She was bound to drive me bonkers right through eternity – and that was just Mother. If you threw Paula into the mix, then fireworks would fly. Hellish fireworks! Keeping my wits about me for all eternity seemed rather tricky from the outset. And eternity looked never-ending; well, it was: a life sentence without the possibility of parole. I had to pause to consider my options. Doubts niggled at the back of my mind: was I ready to plead guilty?

Paula looked like she was. Dying to go. Her transformation was outstanding, and well overdue. She was no longer the tired, used-up skeletal apparition – she was the sweet and cuddly little girl she used to be when her whole life was still ahead of her and she was free to make sensible choices. Fingers crossed, she would make them in the afterlife. It was her last chance. Mother would keep her on the straight and narrow. For one, she would make her have a cooked breakfast every morning, before releasing Paula into the fields of Paradise. Paula would benefit no end from her mum's cooking! Not to mention Mother's firm hand when it would come to Paula's natural predilection for fraternising with Evil (the Garden of Eden's serpent would at last have someone devious enough to play Snakes & Ladders with) and corrupting the Innocent (neither saint nor angel would be spared her advances). But Mother would keep her safe, and fat. There would be no escape from the relative sanity of Mother's middle-class values, for where could Paula run other than to Hell – and she had been there already once.

Things were looking up for Paula. When I saw Dad, I knew things were looking up for Mother as well, for while she was running after Paula, Dad would take care of her. He had clearly forgiven her for all her earthly trespasses and was ready to take her on – once again. He waved to us from the far end of the hospital corridor where the light shone brightly. It looked like a good place to be. Mother agreed. She squealed with delight and bounced about like a bunny on Duracell. It became her in a way because she had regressed even further back in time and was now a ten-year-old tomboy clad in boy's shorts with elasticised braces and grazed knees. Next to her Paula was perfectly in character, looking like a precious little princess with ribbons in her hair and a toothless smile to die for – all innocence revisited.

Mother took mine and Paula's hands, me on the left, Paula on her right, and said her usual, 'Let's go, together, on three. Dad's waiting. One-two-three …'

'JUMP!' Paula and Mother yelled together. But I didn't. I couldn't. A lump grew in my throat and I couldn't say a word. I pulled my hand away. I stole a furtive glance at my bereaved family: Rob was hugging the kids and they were hugging him back. They stood huddled up together, like a herd of hapless sheep without a shepherd. They needed me.

It wasn't just the eternity with Mother and Paula that held me back, but it was the eternity without Rob and the kids. I couldn't just leave them. How would they cope without me? Who would pay the bills? Who would fix the broken toaster? Who would hold the kids to account? Who would make them pick up their dirty socks and put them in the laundry basket? Who, on earth, would tell them how to live their lives? They needed me.

'Georgie, you're no good to them the way you are – a vegetable, no less,' Mother warned me. She sounded and looked a bit ridiculous, she was hardly compelling in her little boy's shorts. I couldn't possibly take her seriously. And I didn't.

'I'll take my chances, Mum. Off you go. Don't make Dad wait.'

'Let's go, Mum,' Paula had to have the last say. 'She won't come. She'd rather be a turnip than come with us.'

They both turned on their heels and glided away. Typically for him, Dad said nothing, but when they weren't looking, he winked at me. Then the three of them walked into the sunset, Dad bringing up the rear.

APPEAL IS GRANTED ...

I must admit I was sulking. After all the drama of my earlier antics when I had almost '*sleeped*' away and given everybody an almighty fright, I changed my mind and decided to stay. It must have been a bit of an anti-climax for all concerned. They had prepared themselves for the worst, held their collective breath while I was supposed to draw my last one – it must have been exhausting. So as soon as Dr Jarzecki declared me a miracle and I was back beeping and puffing through my extensive machinery, everyone had gone home for a good night's sleep in their own beds. I was particularly hopeful Olivia would be spending the night in her own bed, but I didn't take the risk of verifying that in person. I chose to keep my own company and sulk by my own bedside.

On some level it was pleasant: the comforting beeping, the reliable hiss of my ventilator, the reassuring smell of disinfectants, the occasional patter of nurses' feet in the corridor, a random stranded soul asking for directions. I could focus on feeling sorry for myself.

As I was beginning to feel restless (no good sulking without an audience), Tony walked in. The first thought that hit me was that of sheer horror. I looked like shit: no whorish make up, no killer heels, no bucketfuls of *Opium*. Just poor, ailing me, flattened in a hospital bed with tubes sticking out of my nose and plasters stuck to my forehead. I would never allow that to be the last memory of me hovering before Tony's eyes. I had to recover if only to erase that unfortunate picture from his mind.

I was just about to rise from the dead and put on some makeup when he stopped me. He sat on my bedsheets, thus pinning me down. In the past, I would have welcomed that experience with my arms wide opened, drooling at the thought of carnal pleasures to follow.

As it was, I was just drooling.

Tony took my hand. Considering all the invasive intimacies we had shared in the past, he had never held my hand. I wished I could feel it. Both his hands were clasped over mine with some plastic peg protruding between his middle and fore fingers, trying to separate us. Again my wishful thinking kicked in: I wished I could pull that damned peg off. I didn't give a toss if that peg, attached to a fat needle, was what was keeping me alive. I didn't want anything between me and Tony. I wished I could smell his stag scent and sense the heat of his body … All over again, I was working myself up into an orgasm, one which I knew would never come. That's how impotence must feel, I concluded sadly.

He must have sensed my frustration. He patted my hand – a rather disappointingly paternal gesture – and kissed my forehead.

'Sorry it took me so long …' he said.

You were busy, I told him, not that he took any notice.

'… but I was busy'.

You shouldn't have done it! I said, and immediately wanted to kiss him better.

'I shouldn't have done it,' he echoed after me. 'It didn't make any difference. I still feel like crap …'

Try getting into my shoes!

'… and you're still dying.'

Speak for yourself!

'And you'll never know –'

Ha!

'If I told you,' he made his hand into a pistol, pointed at my head and fired, 'I'd have to kill you.'

I'm doing a good job of that myself, thank you very much!

He bent over and only then did I notice he'd brought a bag with him: a Tesco bag. Was he going to smother me with it? Couldn't he wait? I was just about to kick the bucket anyway.

He produced a bunch of grapes. 'Brought you some grapes,' he said and dangled the bunch in the air. Then, one by one, he ate them.

Well, I told myself, *it's the thought that counts.*

He was speaking to me with his mouth full. Perhaps, because of what he was saying, he wanted his words muffled. 'You're such a pain in the arse, Georgie … Why, oh why? Why do I care so much? What the hell is there about you that I love so much? You're just a bloody pain.' At this point I was speechless. I had never heard a confession of love delivered to me with less grace. Come to think, I had never heard a confession of love – full stop. Rob wasn't one for declarations of undying anything.

Then came the punchline.

'I think I'll go away for a while. I can't take this shit.'

And *that* was what got me going. I couldn't let him go, not even for a while. It was my blinking heart again. The bleeping went berserk, lights flashed, steam came out of my ears, and a war cry tore from my chest …

OK. Maybe I'm exaggerating, but what I did, in a nutshell, was to wake up. Or perhaps, more to the point, I came back from the dead.

Since that day when Rob had compressed my chest into a cardiac arrest, which surprisingly had been only a couple of weeks ago, I had lived – vegetated, rather – in fear of there being a funeral soon. And there was. Luckily, it wasn't my own.

Other than that, I wasn't feeling particularly smug about it: after all, it was my mother and my sister who were being laid to rest. Their two coffins had been lowered into the hole in the ground, Mother first, Paula on top, watched by a respectable crowd of mourners.

I was still in a wheelchair, too weak to stand, too shaken up to deliver eulogies. In fact, there were no eulogies. Rob had always been a man of few words, shying away from the spotlight. And even if he wanted to say something about Paula, I didn't want to take the chance of hearing it. Rob couldn't lie and we didn't want the truth to come out. It was better off buried alongside Paula. As for Mother, she wouldn't want us to speak behind her back. She would say, *'Speak to my face, or shut up!'* So we shut up.

Did I mention a crowd? There was one. A cavalcade of raven-black limousines had rolled up, and out of them poured the thespians of Paula's world. They wouldn't miss the opportunity to flash their veiled, wide-brimmed hats and black cloaks, to wipe away theatrical tears with crisp white handkerchiefs that would contrast beautifully with their black leather gloves. I was sure Paula was smiling in her coffin, in the secure knowledge that she could have done grief so much better than the lot of them.

Tony had come, too. With a bouquet of red roses. They didn't look the freshest, I assured myself, a pang of uncharitable jealousy stinging my cardiac-challenged heart. He must've pre-ordered them for my funeral – for me. It would have been such a shame to waste them, so Paula got them in the end. That girl! Once again she was centre stage!

Three months later we were back in court: the lot of us. One happy family. I sat in the gallery – it wasn't my case to run. Next to me was my semi-faithful husband and honorary kettle holder, Rob. Emma held Brandon's hand, or he held hers – whichever way it was, they were holding hands openly and in public, and with my blessing. Mark and Chi delayed their departure to Vietnam to be there for me and see the wheels of justice in motion. Tony was present too, crossing swords with the pimply Gavin

Aitken, the only *persona non grata* in the courtroom.

On reflection, 'crossing swords' is an overstatement. Aitken couldn't cross his fingers when it came to it, so what they were really doing was just congratulating themselves on the conclusion of the case. Jason Mahon had pleaded guilty to theft and two counts of grievous bodily harm under sections 18 and 20 of the Offences Against the Person Act 1861. One of those 'persons' was me and the other Brandon.

Aitken had done his best – which wasn't much, really – to implicate Jason in the killing of Ehler, but Tony had, skilfully, weeded that idea out of Gavin's head, by firstly reminding him of departmental budget cuts and the pressures of running a full-blown trial. Then came the reasonable doubt: there had been no traces of gunpowder on Jason's fingers. The gun used had in fact never been found. Jason confessed to being in Ehler's study, but the fatal shot was fired from the garden. The killer's footprints were size tens while Jason was only a size seven, not to mention that his only footwear was a pair of very tired trainers with a tread not even remotely resembling that of the killer's shoes.

We all sighed relief when Aitken agreed to accept the guilty plea Tony put in front of him on Jason's behalf. Bizarrely, we were all rooting for Jason. After all, he hadn't done it under his own steam. He was a hapless victim in Ehler's schemes, just like the rest of us. Admittedly, he was a shitty little weasel with a lot on his conscience, but then weren't we all in some shape or form? We had to sort of adopt Jason into our small but tight family of misfits and small-time criminals. He sort of grew on us. After all, were we any better than him? Tony, the cold-blooded killer? Brandon, the statutory rapist? Or I, who concealed their deeds, the accessory after the fact on all counts? In comparison, Jason's crimes paled into insignificance. He had only done what he had been told to do: had gone and 'grabbed life by the feet'. How was he to know a more conventional way to go about it? And he didn't get away with it. We did. The least we owed him was the membership of our club.

We had come to court to hear the sentence. We were holding our fingers crossed for our assailant as the judge read his lengthy dictum. Jason, as his weasel's nature dictated, wriggled and fidgeted through the entire process as if his body was under attack by legions of deadly ants. He didn't understand a word of it: not a word about the aggravating circumstances of his crimes which justified placing the offences in Category One, featuring greater culpability; and not a word about the mitigating circumstances being few and far between, his tender age being the most prominent one.

The Honourable Justice Poggycock reduced Jason's sentence to six years following his guilty plea. That was what Jason understood. He knew all about the possibility of parole and so he raised a triumphant fist in the air and cried, 'Yeah!' You would be excused for thinking he had just been nominated for a BAFTA.

We were happy for him. He was now a serious criminal, not a petty car thief as he had been at the start of his adventure, but an offender of great standing in the criminal community, a man who could kill if pushed. No one would dare try his patience in prison. Jason was a crime lord in the making. In a way, he really had grabbed life by its feet.

But more to the point, it had never really been about Jason. We left the courtroom, carrying our sins with us. In a way, we all got away with murder.

It's been a few years since it all happened. Only now did I manage to write it all down for posterity. Before I put this memoir away in a safe place with instructions for it to be opened fifty years after my death, I need to say that had it been written by someone else I would not believe a word of it. Sometimes I have to pinch myself to believe it. Like the other day when I bumped into Etienne in court.

I said, 'Etienne? What brings you here?'

He went white as a sheet. His lip trembled as he finally managed to stagger over his dodgy past to correct me.

'My name is Jack Raulston ... I'm a forensic psychologist. I'm an expert witness for the defence.'

'Of course. Sorry, I mistook you for someone else,' I mumbled hopelessly.

Tony, the defence counsel in that case, gaped wide-mouthed for a good minute or two after overhearing my faux pas.

Oh well, shit happens. I am glad to know that Etienne – or Jack, Tony got that one right! – has made something of himself.

Mark is doing well too. He has become something of a romantic hero – a Don Quixote fighting the windmills of injustice in the remote outposts of the Far East, with Chi, his very own Sancho Panza, by his side. The apple could not have fallen further away from the tree because Rob still delights in gardening and reading on the bus.

Emma, having read History for no particular reason whatsoever, joined forces with Brandon to open their own restaurant. It is called *The Jurassic Roast* – an allusion to the size of their portions, not their freshness, I assume. It was either a restaurant or a lifetime of unemployment for the pair of them. I think they've made the right choice.

Olivia has become a cherished family friend, valued especially for her cooking abilities. We always invite her for Christmas dinner. I must confess I watch her chubby little chorizos very carefully whenever they stray too closely to my husband. Like they say: keep your friends close and your enemies even closer.

Finally, to Tony. Unlike Olivia, he has not become a cherished family friend. He lives dangerously somewhere on the periphery of my respectable existence. That is the best I can wish for because I know I wouldn't be able to keep my hands off him.

Not to mention the fact that he can't cook.

THE END

More Accent Press Thrillers

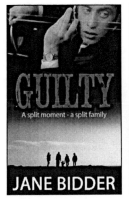

For more information about **Anna Legat**
and other **Accent Press** titles
please visit

www.accentpress.co.uk

Lightning Source UK Ltd.
Milton Keynes UK
UKOW02f2304020615

252794UK00001B/6/P